Uncle Chris's Collection of Crafty Short Stories

By P. Frost

Can you work out the twist?

Published by New Generation Publishing in 2024

Copyright © P. Frost 2024

First Edition

The author asserts the moral right under the Copyright, Designs and Patents Act 1988 to be identified as the author of this work.

All Rights reserved. No part of this publication may be reproduced, stored in a retrieval system or transmitted, in any form or by any means without the prior consent of the author, nor be otherwise circulated in any form of binding or cover other than that which it is published and without a similar condition being imposed on the subsequent purchaser.

ISBN: 9781835635056

New Generation Publishing
www.newgeneration-publishing.com

The Twenty Short Stories

1	The Manuscript
2	The Romantic Pub Rendezvous
3	Brothers in Arms
4	The Earl and his Grandsons
5	Sights and Sounds
6	A Bridge Between Life and Death
7	The Lone Youngster on the Boundary
8	The Perfect Steal
9	An Unlikely Witness
10	So Who Did It?
11	Tools of the Trade
12	The Greek Artefact
13	The Train Journey
14	Did You Hear About the Burglary?
15	Eating like a Gannet
16	A Smile Means Everything
17	Caught in the Act
18	The Lifeguard
19	Office Life
20	Nurses Knows Best

Introduction

Welcome to Uncle Chris's Collection of Crafty Short Stories.

As you have bought this book you are obviously keen to read short stories that are interesting and have an unexpected twist.

Here you will find a collection of very short stories. See if you can work out the unexpected finale of each story before you get to the end of it. By the time you get to the last two stories of the book you will see how Uncle Chris fools even his own brothers grandchildren!

Preface

It was another bitterly cold dark winter's night high up in the snowy Welsh mountains. Uncle Chris, sitting in front of his roaring log fire, was enjoying the many delights of his huge, secluded luxury log cabin, which was situated next to a lonely tarn, halfway up one of the highest and coldest mountains in Wales.

Uncle Chris's favourite moment was sitting in his expansive leather armchair in front of the evening log fire, with supporting lit candles all around the floor providing the only light for the large room. This gave him the ambience he wanted to read his twisty stories to his favourite guests.

With him in his log cabin were Ash and Sandy, the two young grandchildren of his younger brother. He was of course technically a Great Uncle to the youngsters, but they simply called him Uncle Chris.

Now a retired Physiotherapist, Uncle Chris could spend a little of his retirement time with the two grandchildren, and this weekend it was to be a few days for the three of them together in the luxury chalet. Both grandchildren were fit and athletic teenagers; a relief for Uncle Chris as so many offspring nowadays waste away sitting unhealthily in front of a computer. Ash was the school's first eleven cricket captain and a prolific fast bowler. Sandy was a schools county champion in both chess and badminton. They were clever, outgoing children indeed, and both loved listening to evening stories from Uncle Chris while sitting in the dim light of the roaring chalet fire.

The two children now sat opposite Uncle Chris in front of the fire having finished their supper. They knew about his cunningly created stories and never got the twist at the end. He had crafted them carefully and tested them on Jade, his gorgeous wife. She had a sharp-witted brain and had finetuned them, so now the stories were ready to spring on the grandchildren. A while ago Uncle Chris compiled the stories in a book and was now ready to dramatically read them out to the youngsters in the glow of the fireside. They had to work out what the ending would be before he himself got to the end of the story. They were always fooled by his stories.

Uncle Chris had written twenty stories for this book. He had time tonight for two stories to read to them before bedtime. It would be the last two stories in this book that he would read to the children, but do read the first eighteen beforehand..........

Short Story 1: The Manuscript

It is the winter of 1903 and a very testing time for both the rich and the poor. Harsh winters and feeble harvests have meant that food is lacking for everyone, especially for the poor. For the rich, life is starting to change following the recent death of Queen Victoria.

The Duke of Tinsdale is a very rich man. He is a clever businessman and has made his fortune over the years, resulting in Queen Victoria rewarding him with a beautiful abbey to reside in with his family. He lives with his beautiful wife and three children, all girls, in a huge Berkshire abbey which sits within an enormous estate which includes a deer park. The estate is so large that it would take a visitor travelling in a typical horse and carriage ten minutes to get to the abbey once they had entered the boundary gates of the estate, such is the long and scenic drive to the abbey. Life is very comfortable in the abbey but there are some concerns for the family. The main one is the huge cost of rectifying the sizable hole in the leaking roof, and the Duke simply hasn't the money to fix it. This perplexes his girls constantly as it is cold and damp in some of the rooms. The Duke always does the right thing for his girls, so he must get this fixed soon.

The Duke and his wife are both very private people, in contrast to his three girls who are all outspoken, very pretty, a little spoilt and are very determined young adults.

The eldest daughter Celia is a passionate journalist and now lives and works in London. She always dresses smartly, usually in blue, and captures the eyes of those around her. Nancy is the Duke's youngest daughter and is also his favourite. Her slender appearance and brunette hair captured the eyes of the Earl of Liverpool some time ago so she spends her time travelling north to see her beloved. Joy, the middle of the Duke's three daughters is a studious, determined writer. Her works have been inspired by the novels of Jane Austen. She is the shortest of the three and while she doesn't capture the attention of many potential suitors she is determined to be successful in everything she does, even at the expense of others.

The Duke and his family are served by a team of service staff, which includes a head butler, under butler, facilities manager, cook and two young kitchen serving girls. Smithers, the head butler, rules the service team with a rod of iron and an emotionless manner. His view is woe betide anyone for making mistakes, stepping out of line, or disrespecting the Duke. The Duke has inherited his staff recently from a nearby Mansion where the incumbent Baron had recently retired. He now wants to get to know his new staff as he had only been introduced to them once before and doesn't know any of them very well. However, protocol for the upper class in the early 1900's means that contact with service staff isn't the done thing for the Duke and his family. Instead, staff are meant to be seen and not heard. The Duke knows that times are changing for the upper classes since the Queens death, and he is keen to implement some new contemporary ideas into the abbey, which, as far as he is concerned includes getting to know his staff well and gaining their respect. He hoped to see them as an extension to his family rather than a set of slaves and he is very keen to make this happen, especially for the cook and the two vulnerable kitchen girls Elsie and Betty, who he understands are regularly badly treated by Smithers. Last Friday the Duke secretly gave Betty some money to enjoy a Friday night with her friends; a simple sign that working life in the abbey would improve for the staff in future.

One morning, and to start his new era of being more personable to his employees, the Duke simply walks into the kitchen without warning Smithers, who now wears a worried expression on his forehead, as this is not the norm; he is now not in control. The staff all stop working in the kitchen and either bow or curtsy to the Duke. He waves them all to relax and asks them to sit down at the huge communal kitchen table so he could have a few words with everyone. After a short introduction to the new team the Duke then asks for and completes a two minute private one-to-one chat with each member of staff. By doing this he learns their names and a little about them. The short meetings were useful but on later reflection he was disappointed that the staff did not have much to say. However, one of the young kitchen serving girls, Elsie, told him that she was eighteen this month and her hobby is writing stories and novels. The Duke found this fascinating as his own daughter Joy also liked to write, so he probed further with questions for Elsie, and as he did so he was taken by Elsie's calm and engaging manner. She was a little flustered at the extra questions that the Duke had for her but was glad that the Duke showed interest in the recent manuscript that she had drafted. The Duke eventually called all the staff together and gave his thanks for their time. He ended the team meeting by asking Elsie to bring his midday coffee into his study in a few minutes time.

The Duke is now in his study and as Elsie enters the room with coffee he calls her over to his desk and asks her a few more questions about her writing. He realises that both Elsie and his daughter Joy seem to enjoy writing in similar genres, and he then asks Elsie what she plans to do with her stories. Elsie tells him that she would love to publish her manuscript as a book but does not know how to go about doing it. Of course she doesn't know how, he thinks, she is a mere kitchen girl who doesn't look after her self well. She might be bright in the head but her unkempt hair and lack of attention to her appearance does not help her much in life.

The Duke ponders on Else's conundrum. His daughter Joy also wants to publish a novel which she also has in manuscript form, but Joy has the useful connection of her sister Celia, who is a journalist and mixes with publishers every day. The Duke offers to read Elsie's manuscript and promises to offer her his opinion on her book. Elsie jumps at this idea and hopes that the Duke might help her progress it. She doesn't know that his daughter also writes novels and the Duke decides not to tell her this. Elsie is now very keen to hand over her manuscript to him to read, and hopes he might think of a way to help her.

Two weeks later a nervous Elsie brings her finished manuscript in and secretly gives it to the Duke while she brings him morning coffee. She does not tell the other service staff that she enjoys writing or that she has brought the novel for the Duke to read as she knows she should not really mingle with the Duke and his family. Besides, Smithers would be angry at her if he found out that she was going over his head and talking to the head of the household, which is not the done thing.

The Duke gives his thanks to Elsie for the manuscript while they are alone in his study and when Else leaves the room untidily he reads it quickly. It does not take him long to realise that Elsie's novel is excellent, with colourful characters and an engaging plot. This contrasts with his daughter's novel which he read yesterday. He was disappointed with it as Joy's work was poorly constructed and lacked excitement. Joy had asked her father yesterday to take her manuscript to London one day, in order that her sister Celia could persuade her publisher friends to launch her novel.

The Duke now has two novels on his desk. One is from his daughter Joy, which is poor and another from Elsie, his kitchen serving girl, which is excellent. He knows Joy will be heartbroken if she knew Elsie not only writes but has a better story to publish. The Duke flicks through both manuscripts again and ponders to himself. He looks at the novel from his daughter and sees that Joy has signed her name at the bottom, and then he looks at the other manuscript and sees that Elsie has also signed her own name at the bottom of it. He then puts them both in his briefcase.

Two days later the Duke travels to London to meet Celia

travelling there using his own horse and carriage. Joy is aware of this trip but Elsie is not. On the way he looks out of the carriage window, past the leading horses of the carriage and admires the view across the Berkshire countryside. This country has miles of open land. A few minutes later he sees a lame stag lying by the roadside. It has been snared by a trap and must have been there for some time and the stag is near death. If he tells his three girls that he simply left it there in agony, they would be upset. The Duke always does the right thing for his girls so he stops the carriage, pulls out his musket, and puts the stag out of his misery.

He continues his journey to London to visit Celia in her office building which is full of journalists and publishers, and he soon arrives at her company office. He greets his daughter and is surprised at her aloof, snobbish manner. It must be her preferred work style he thinks. She has dressed well, again wearing light blue. With the Duke are the two manuscripts from his daughter Joy and serving girl Elsie sitting comfortably in his briefcase. However, a few minutes earlier while Celia was showing her father around the offices Celia had mentioned that the publishers tend only to publish one book a year. The Duke hasn't told Celia yet that he has two manuscripts, the one from Joy and the other from Elsie. Now that he knows only one manuscript can be published the Duke has to decide which one to hand over to Celia.

While he is considering his decision Celia suddenly asks him if he has Joys manuscript for her. The Duke does have it but he secretly knows that Joys novel is poor and doesn't want her to be ridiculed by Celia's colleagues. He replies in the affirmative and slowly brings out one of the manuscripts, the one with Elsie's name on it. He must now explain to Celia who Elsie is, and that she has a better novel than Joy. He knows that Celia will explode on finding out that he prefers a mere kitchen girl to have her book published instead of her sister.

He passes to Celia Elsie's manuscript and expects a verbal explosion. Instead, he gets a surprising smile. Celia chuckles and says that she is impressed that Joy wants to use the pseudonym "Elsie", rather than her own name. She reckons this would mean that Joy will get genuine acclaim rather than using her family contacts to secure a publishing contract. The Duke breathes a sigh of relief as Celia doesn't realise that Elsie is in fact a kitchen girl and it is her work he is giving to Celia and not Joy's.

Celia invites a smartly dressed publisher friend to come into the office with them and they speed-read the manuscript while her father has some coffee. When they finish, the publisher tells him that this novel is superb and will sell millions of copies while making the author very rich. Celia smiles to her father as she knows that Joy would then easily be able to pay for the leaking abbey roof, and also make her father proud. She is pleased that her father has brought the novel to her and she knows that the Duke always does the right thing for his girls. The Duke returns Celia's smile.

On the way home the Duke sits in his carriage while the horses do the hard work to transport him back to the abbey. The rhythmical sway of the carriage almost sends him to sleep but his thoughts keep him awake. He is now in deep thought and has to work out what to say to Joy, because in a few months time when she see's the first draft of her novel, she will find out that it isn't her work that she is reading but instead a completely different novel from someone else. The Duke remembers that Elsie the kitchen girl doesn't know that he has been to London with her work.

The following month was the worst month in the Dukes life. His wife was diagnosed with cancer early in the month, and then a week later he got the call that all fathers dread. A train crash on the Reading line had killed ten people, one of which was Joy, who was travelling to Reading to buy some new clothes for an upcoming evening ball. The funeral two weeks later was heart-breaking for the Duke and his family. Of course, he organised the perfect funeral for his daughter; the Duke always does the right thing for his girls.

It took a few months for the Duke to come to terms with recent events.

One morning while he was having his mid-morning coffee in the study the Duke received a formal letter from his daughter Celia from her company in London. She had written to say that Joy's manuscript had gone down well with the publishers, the Elsie pseudonym was a masterstroke, the edits were complete and the book was now ready to print.

With all the emotion over his wife's situation and Joy's death, the Duke had forgotten about the manuscript. He had let Celia and her publishing company think that Joy was using a pseudonym, whereas he knew that the manuscript was really Elsie's work.

Then it occurred to the Duke that no one knew that Elsie had written the novel that he gave to Celia as nobody had seen either Elsie's or Joy's manuscript before he gave it to Celia, other than him. Elsie would probably not find out soon; he hadn't told her that he had taken her manuscript to London, so she would only find out if she bought the book when it was published, which was unlikely with her meagre wages.

The Duke read the rest of the letter. Celia advised her father to have a book launch for selected V.I.P's at Tinsdale Abbey as it would be a wonderful venue to invite special guests and publicise the book, which he agreed to.

The summer of 1904 is now approaching and on a hot June afternoon the Tinsdale Abbey lawn is hosting a large gathering to celebrate the launch of the book. It is the first time that the specially invited guests will get their hands on the novel, which had been widely acclaimed by the publisher in the press over the last few weeks.

The Duke has been asked by Celia to make a speech to all gathered on the lawn before the pre-launch books are distributed to the large crowd. After the event these well-connected guests will use their web of connections to publicise the book and when the book hits the shops it will inevitably sell well. The guests include politicians, the clergy and high powered business folk so it is important that the day goes well.

It is now mid-afternoon on the special day. The weather is warm, perfect for a summer party. Celia helps the Duke to host the event and she looks resplendent in her dark blue suit. Everyone present have dressed smartly. Celia stands with a glass of champagne while standing on the lawn commanding everybody's attention. She watches her father grab the loud haler and make a speech in honour of Joys book. Over a hundred people are present on the lawn, including the Dukes other daughter Nancy, and his wife, who's health has somewhat improved over the last few weeks. Also in the crowd are the staff; Smithers, the under butler, the facility manager, the cook and the two young kitchen serving girls, one of which is Elsie, who still doesn't realise that the book contains her work and not Joy's. The Dukes service staff have set up this afternoons event well and kept everyone fed and watered superbly. The Duke is suitably proud of them as they stand to one side of the assembled guests in their black and white uniforms.

The Duke gets up to speak and welcomes everyone to the event, praising his new staff for setting up the lawn admirably. He refers to them proudly as an extension to his family.

Then he thanks his daughter Celia for organising publication of the book and for her valuable comments during the editing stage. The Duke then tells everyone how impressed he is by the quality of the novel, which will be handed out in a few minutes time. He tells all present that the publishers advise that the novel will easily sell millions of books.

It is only then that he discloses to those who have gathered on the lawn that the term "Elsie" in the novel is not a pseudonym for his daughter Joy, but is the name of the actual book author and that she is present on the lawn today. He looks over to Elsie Smith, a mere scruffy kitchen girl, standing alongside the other staff and smiles at her as she and the crowd now realise what is happening.

His wife and Celia have a look of horror on their faces.

Elsie's face turns white in shock as it suddenly dawns on her that everyone is looking at her and she now understands what is going on as the Duke has actually been talking about her work and not Joy's. She realises that the Duke has just said that her book would sell millions, so she will be richer than anyone gathered here. She might be more famous than Jane Austin.

The Duke smiles at Elsie the kitchen girl. He always does the right thing for his girls.

Short Story 2: The Romantic Pub Rendezvous

Shane has just arrived at the local pub on a wintry Saturday evening. He is on his own tonight. No lads, no friends, no family, just him, and he reckons that he looks dressed to kill. He is looking very sharp in his new chinos, trendy shirt, shiny black shoes and armed with the latest smartphone. His shoes are cheap, he bought them from a discount shop earlier in the day, but he does wear them well and he feels good. Recent redundancy from his bricklaying job means that he has to be careful of money, but tonight is the night to have fun. A short hair cut this morning allows him to be ready for romance in the pub tonight. He is in a particularly good mood after he and two rowdy mates went to see his football team, West Ham, win earlier in the day. The game was exciting and of course it is always good when your team wins. A pie and a pint for lunch was a good way to start the day at the football. He didn't tell the lads about what he might be up to this evening though.

He now buys a cocktail at the trendy bar. Cocktails impress all who might be looking for fun, he thinks. He looks around at all the young people present this evening. Everyone is sharply dressed, but then so is he, and he sits at the bar waiting for his moment.

This might a small pub but it is well known for its trendy punters and lively music. It is also convenient for Shane as it's only a short walk from home. As he consumes his first drink of the evening his thoughts turn to romance. Shane is the type of bloke who has always preferred blonds. All his past female liaisons had been blond haired girls. He now sits and waits for a blond to walk through the door. While sitting at the bar he keeps an eye on the entrance door to see who arrives.

Surprisingly, who should walk in right now but his best buddy from his old bricklaying job. Normally that would be a great opportunity for a good evening but tonight he is after romance and not a lad's night out. His buddy greets him with a typical loud high five and then comments on Shanes trendy clothes. Shane wants to get rid of him quickly and is relieved that his friend is keen to walk on past him, and as he passes Shane his friend joins the lads playing snooker.

Shane orders another cocktail while sitting at the bar and while it is being created a pretty brunette girl called Tracey who he has never seen before walks into the pub. She has a lovely figure and walks past Shane without even a look in his direction and then mixes with the snooker boys.

It is not long before the entrance door is opened again, but this time in walks a mullet haired man with a guitar case. He is clearly playing with the live band tonight and as the man walks past Shane the man enjoys the looks from the many girls as he makes his way to the stage to join the band.

Then, while Shane finishes his second drink, a blond walks through the front door and into the pub. Petula is greeted by one of the lads near the door. She replies and is very well spoken. She is a blond with long glossy hair and looks top class. A perfect figure, warm smile and bubbly personality. Shane thinks Petula looks great, but she simply walks straight past him with only a slight furtive glance in his direction. Her fragrance trails behind her. It is Bloom Eau Parfum, Shanes favourite. She makes her way to the other end of the bar knowing that Shane has picked up her scent.

A young lad at the far end of the bar gets to Petula and quickly chats her up. He is called Sebastian and appears very slick with a neat chat up line. After asking for her name he continues to use it in every sentence he utters, which annoys Shane as he listens in to the conversation. It also annoys Shane that Petula appears to enjoy the attention of Sebastian, who hasn't made the effort to dress well, but soon she tires of Sebastian and walks away to a vacant table. He smiles. Now he is ready.

As she sits down at the table she quickly glances at Shane. He likes that "come and get me" glance, so he wanders over to Petula's table in as cool a manner as he can and starts a conversation.

Shane comes from a working class background where mum and dad struggled to make ends meet so Shane has to make the best of the very little that he has. His social skills are not perfect but he is a good looker and decent conversationalist which has helped him in the past with the ladies. He looks at Petula across the table. She looks fabulous and dresses well. She offered to pay for some drinks, but Shane won't have that; he doesn't mind being a little bit sexist in this case.

Shane asks Petula about her day. Petula describes her day in detail and in particular the difficult time that she had at work dealing with some marketing clients who earlier visited her company's elite office in London's Canary Wharf. Shane then told Petula about his day, the football with the lads, applying for another brick laying job, then getting ready for this evening's visit to the pub.

The conversation at the table continues with many smiles and after an hour Petula suggests a walk. The pub is adjacent to the Thames, so they take a walk alongside the river. It is a particularly beautiful stretch of the river so a walk would be wonderful.

As they talk they link arms together and give each other deep, meaningful eye contact. There is some serious chemistry going on now.

Shane decides it is time to change the subject and suggests what he and Petula might do later tonight. Petula smiles to herself, Shane isn't going to waste time walking by the river anymore. The old man who is walking his dog beside the river a few yards behind them hears their conversation and is left in no doubt what these two people are going to get up to later tonight. He takes a turn to the right, to let them walk on ahead and enjoy their walk alone.

Out of the blue Petula asks Shane the classic question "Do you want to come back to my place?" in that pretending seedy tone of voice that you only hear in television programs. She says this and then with her eyes she clearly suggests what would happen back at the house. She knows that he won't resist.

When they get to the house Petula opens the front door. She hopes the house is empty, it was when she left it. Petula quickly checks that no one has come home unexpectedly. After a quick search in all the downstairs rooms she smiles and leads Shane by the arm upstairs. Petula opens her bedroom and they both go in; she then closes it tight shut. They begin to get to know each other intimately.

When all is done, and they are lying together in bed recovering, Petula hears the dreaded front door open with a squeak. She is shocked and panics. She thought the house would be empty tonight and didn't think that he would return so quickly. Petula and Shane hurriedly get their clothes back on. Just as they finish getting dressed the bedroom door opens and Victor stands and stares at them both, with a horrified expression on his face. Petula is crestfallen. The last thing she wanted was for Victor to see her like this.

Victor shakes his head and tells his mum that she is fifty-five years old and should know better than to get caught out like this.

Then Victor turns to Shane and tells his dad that he is two years older than mum and should be leading by example.

Then Victor remembers. It is mum and dads twenty eighth wedding anniversary today and every anniversary evening they re-enact their first ever meeting in the local pub.

Victor shakes his head again. Mums and dads can be so embarrassing.

Short Story 3: Brothers In Arms.

No matter what people tell you no one ever gets fooled by a set of identical twins.

We have all heard the stories. Some of us have even seen an identical twin pair, and of course they can appear extremely similar, but we have never really mistaken one twin for the other, even if they do appear very similar. There are stories where people get duped but I don't think it happens in real life. All these stories are very unlikely as even the most identical of twins will have slightly different characters, manners or postures. Any of these differences will catch them out if they try to trick other people.

Steve and Tom are identical twins who live in New York. It is now the early 2000's and a few years ago when they were at school they never dreamed of using their similarities to play tricks on girlfriends, for the simple reason that from the age of six they disliked each other intensely and never communicated at all. They were so similar to each other in personality as well as looks that they couldn't get on and argued constantly. When they left school and got employment, they did live close by but never contacted each other. Now, they only speak when necessary.

Even though they are almost identical in appearance there are some personality differences in the two brothers. Steve is the more successful of the two. He married his school girlfriend Judy only a year or so ago, just before the new millennium celebrations. He is well paid so they both enjoy a big house and plenty of money to spend outside of work. All seems well, at least to them. Judy loves music and is a massive Jimi Hendrix fan. So, to impress her while on holiday Steve learned how to play the national anthem on his guitar using his teeth to pluck the strings, just like Jimi Hendrix used to do. Now, on every holiday, he does this party trick with his teeth to impress both her and the friends they are with on holiday. It's bonkers really but it makes them both laugh. Just two months ago they were on a business trip to South Africa where, after doing a presentation to the host company, he performed his musical party trick, to tumultuous applause from their hosts. They absolutely loved it, especially as everyone had had a drink or two.

While Steve is doing well, his twin brother Tom however, is struggling with life. He might look like Steve, but he does not have Steve's business acumen. He hates music, and struggles both financially and with most of his relationships. Tom does have a cheap flat in New York, but the rent is steep, and he can only just get by. He still won't talk to Steve and is very jealous of how Steve is now doing well in life since leaving school, while he himself struggles. It seems these brotherly wounds won't heal.

However, soon after Steve and Judy's South African business trip the couple talk one day, and Judy persuades Steve to talk to Tom to try to at least be on talking terms. Steve is not keen to contact his brother, but Judy keeps trying to persuade her man to make amends with his brother. Judy is a girl from a big happy family herself, so she is keen to see harmony in her husband's family. At last, she can see Steve melting and he agrees to talk to his brother. He contacts Tom and they agree to meet for a coffee and try to be amicable.

He contacted Tom on the phone on 10th September 2001 and they agreed to meet the following day at the coffee area in the base of one the New York World Trade Centre Twin Towers. Unfortunately, the meet is on 11th September 2001 and on this day the two towers fall to the ground killing thousands of people. It is a terrible day for the world. The disaster results in the demise of Steve and Judy, but Tom just makes it out of the building and some kind person rescues him and gets him to safety before the main body of the building falls to the ground. By the afternoon of this fated day he is in hospital and needs hospital treatment, but the important thing is that he survived and after three days in hospital he is allowed to return to his flat. The problem for Tom is that it's not his flat that he has keys for. Instead of possessing his own keys, he has Steve's house keys in his pocket. He cannot understand how this has happened and thinks back to those horrific minutes before the tragedy. He now pieces it together. In the dash for safety, as the tower disintegrated, everybody in the cafe grabbed their belongings and ran for dear life, but in the confusion, Tom accidentally took Steve's keys from the coffee table and Steve took his keys. So now Tom can't get into his own flat as he has the wrong keys, but he can get in Steve house instead and Steve died a day or so ago.

As Tom leaves the hospital in the back of the taxi he thinks through his options now that he has the keys to his brother's plush home and smiles to himself. Tom has a much bigger and better home than he does, with many valuable material items in it. Tom arrives at Steve's huge house and pays the taxi driver. He quickly gets in Steve's house with the unexpected keys that he now has and starts to enjoy the luxury within the house.

Tom knows that he is not in Steve's will, as they have not got on well, so he will not benefit from Steve's death. Tom is poor but he is not stupid. Yes, he does have a thought about impersonating his rich brother, but he will be found out easily if he decides to live here and attempt to convince the neighbours that he is Steve. He will surely be found out after a few days. So instead, Tom has a look around his brother's posh house to see if he can pick a few useful things up. He will then take them to his flat and use them there. If a neighbour sees him in this posh house they will think, from a distance, that he is Steve. No one will know yet that Steve has perished; that will probably take a few days.

In the house, he see's many material items that he could pinch. Televisions, sofas, music equipment all look interesting. However, he is taken by a letter that he sees on

Steve's desk. It's from the South African company that Steve visited recently with Judy. They have thanked him for his financial contribution to set the company up and as a thank you they have invited him to come to South Africa and have a two-week holiday in a top hotel nearby and receive, as a gift, one of their valuable diamonds that have come from the mine that the company's owns. Tom had heard about this trip from Judy when he spoke to her recently. She told him all about the trip including details about the company and how charming the employees were.

Well, Tom finds this a very interesting letter to read. A quick impersonation of Steve would give Tom a nice holiday in South Africa and a valuable diamond that he could sell and make some money from. If he went there impersonating his brother he would easily get away with it as the people Steve met were only in contact with Steve for a short while and it has been a few months since the visit now so they won't notice any minor differences in their appearance or manner. He could make excuses for why Judy couldn't come and then enjoy a mini holiday and top up his bank account with money made from the diamond, after selling it on the black market. No-one would be the wiser. By the time the South African company find out about Steve's demise Tom would have the diamond in his possession and be gone.

Tom writes and replies on Steve's behalf accepting the invitation, while giving an excuse for why Judy can't come.

Various arrangements are made by Tom and very soon all is set for his trip. He now has Steve's clothes, after-shave and travel bags. He travels on his own passport but also takes Steve's passport with him in case the hotel asks for it. The only people who need to be convinced that he looks like Steve are the people in the company who have only seen him once or twice, so he should be able to get away with it.

Tom travels to South Africa. The hotel is stupendous, first class everything. Food, recreation and an evening massage are wonderful. They have a spa where he can take a massage and a swim (and minimise the amount of time that he is seen by people in general). Tom looks forward to tonight's final evening event where he will meet the company's staff and receive their thanks for the money that Steve had provided for them. He particularly looks forward to the very end of the evening where he will receive the priceless diamond. Before all this though he opens the mini bar in his room and cracks open a beer. His plan is working well. He imagines how the evening will go. It will start with a company drinks party for the company staff at the hotel. Two of the company's directors will meet Tom in the bar and they will have cocktails together. Tom gets ready and makes sure he is as Steve-like as possible in all aspects of his appearance and behaviour. He then makes his way down to the hotel bar and greets the two directors.

One of them obviously liked Steve a lot as he is incredibly gracious to Tom and can't do enough to make him comfortable. The other director cracks a joke, which Tom doesn't understand. It's a joke that Steve and the director shared a few months ago so the man is surprised that Tom doesn't smile. He now becomes suspicious of Tom, and then even more so because Judy isn't with him. Steve had told the director when they met last time that he wouldn't go anywhere without her. His suspicions grow as the evening progresses. He now remembers Judy telling him that Steve has an identical brother, but no one talks about him as they don't get along. He wanders if this man in front of him is an imposter.

The two directors leave Steve for a moment to check arrangements for the diamond ceremony. As they do this the concerned director tells the other director of his suspicions. The other one laughs and suggests that his colleague is paranoid, but then he thinks again. The person that he met today looks like Steve but he shook his hand when they met today, whereas last month Steve was a big open arms hugger when they met. There were a few other differences to the way he behaves now compared to when they last met. The director now joins in his colleagues' suspicions.

They go to talk to Grace who is one of the junior managers. She had also met Steve when he visited a few months ago. Grace befriended Judy at this time and Grace now concurs with the director's concerns. Judy had told Grace about Steve's twin and Grace now agrees that the person who calls himself Steve today might look like Steve from the previous visit but doesn't behave like it now. Besides, he didn't give her a hug today when she met him. She enjoyed that last time. She does have a picture of Steve in her office but can't remember it in detail just now. Perhaps this man is an imposter.

Grace tells the two directors that there is only one way to find out if the man here today who calls himself Steve is real, or is being impersonated, and she leaves quickly. The two directors go back to join Tom and enjoy their drinks together.

The two directors are blunt and ask Tom how his twin brother at home is?

Tom is taken aback. He is concerned now that they are all suspicious, but he has started this mission and so he must continue and blag his way through it. After all, he returns home tomorrow morning, so he doesn't have long to impersonate Steve. The two directors now change their manner and are friendly again with him. Tom is relieved.

Grace comes back to the group and the four of them pleasantly chat.

Suddenly, one of the directors looks at Tom and says defiantly that they all think that he is an imposter and suspects that he is not Steve, but instead his twin brother. Grace stares at Tom and says that she agrees with the two directors. She says that Tom can leave tomorrow and take the diamond, but only on one condition. Tom asks what the condition is.

Grace leans back, picks something up from behind her then looks into his eyes and asks Tom to play his national anthem using his only teeth. She passes him the guitar.

Tom hates music and looks at her with a face which tells them that he has no clue what's going on. Tom doesn't know about Steve's guitar party trick.

Grace and the directors look at each other and smile smugly.

They have him now.

He can't be Steve and he sure isn't going to have a diamond.

Short Story 4: The Earl and his Grandsons

The Earl of Watmoreshire, now a tired man in his eighties, sat in his lounge one winter evening, as the snow settled on the frozen ground outside the abbey. Charles, his new butler, had already lit the fire in the enormous hearth, which had now taken hold and the heat was keeping him comfortably warm while he sat in his cosy armchair.

While supping an expensive whisky the Earl stared into the flickering flames of the fire and thought about how difficult life had been over the last few years while living alone in his Abbey, with just his butler for company. The death of his son in that tragic car crash last year meant that his only surviving family were now his two grandchildren, Harry and Sam. They were now in their late teens and lived with their adopted mother in her cottage only a few miles away from the Earls enormous abbey estate.

The Earl stirred as the lounge door opened, letting cool air into the room, and into the room walked his stone-faced butler, who had brought another whiskey on the rocks for him. Charles had been with the Earl for only a few weeks but had settled in quickly and was a very well organised sole. He looked after the Earl's every needs with quiet, solemn loyalty. He wore the classic butlers black suit with white bowtie and white gloves. Quite the old-fashioned butler.

When Charles left the room the Earl took a sip of his drink and looked over at the small locked wooden case sitting on the table at the far end of the room. The small elegant oak box had a bespoke lock as the contents of the box were extremely valuable. It contained the first Victoria Cross ever to have been made, which had been awarded to one of the Earl's ancestors. Its value was somewhere in the millions of pounds. The lock consisted of a simple four digit code and only the Earl, the two boys and the butler knew the code. The prize possession inside the box was relatively safe in the Abbey as the building security system was first class. You would have to be invited into the abbey to have a chance of stealing anything in the building. The paintings hanging on the walls of each room were all valuable but none of them were as highly valued as the Victoria cross. The Earl was a private man and the only visitors he ever had were his two grandchildren, Harry and Sam. Their adopted mother never visited; she didn't like the Earl as he had omitted the two boys from his will.

Sam and Harry lived with mum in a modest cottage a short walk from the abbey. They might only be young teenagers but they had already fallen fowl of the law and they weren't particularity civil people, unlike their grandfather who was a quintessential English gentleman. The two boys also knew the value of the Earl's Victoria Cross and had plans to steal it. They were those kinds of lads. Stealing the cross would be easy to accomplish for them as they could access the abbey quite easily and they both knew the code for the wooden box. That evening in their cottage they agreed that one of them would steal the cross, especially as the challenge was laid on a plate for them as grandad had recently asked them both to supper the following week. Strangely, the supper invite with grandad was for two separate evenings. Harry would visit on the Saturday night and Sam on the Sunday night. They had been told that the reason for these separate supper meetings was that the Earl wanted to explain to them individually why they were not part of his will.

While Harry and Sam ate tea that evening in the cottage they talked through how they would approach the two evenings. Harry was always the competitive sort and challenged Sam to see which of them could distract the Earl and then open the locked wooden case to steal the cross. They both agreed to try to do the steal when they individually met the Earl. The challenge was accepted by Sam.

Saturday evening soon arrived and Harrys had the first chance to meet grandad for supper and see if he could accomplish the mission. As it was snowing Harry put on his big warm coat and gloves and made his way to the abbey for the supper. When he arrived at the abbey Charles provided a drink for him and he talked with the Earl privately in the lounge, while being warmed by the roaring fire. Harry was convinced that he would beat Sam to steal the cross, especially as he had the first chance to meet Grandad. Sam would have to wait until the next day. The Earl was pleased to have Harry to supper and over the course of the evening they talked about the will and also what Harry had been up to recently. After about an hour the Earl was wary of leaving Harry alone in the lounge for a few minutes while he went to the toilet, but on the Earls return Harry was still sitting in the same seat as when he left, so the Earl felt that all was well with the cross.

At the end of the evening when Harry left the Abbey for home the Earl sat back in his armchair in front of the fire with whiskey in hand and glanced at the wooden box at the far end of the room. Had Harry opened it while he went to the toilet earlier? The Earl wasn't sure but didn't have chance to ponder on this because he soon fell asleep in his armchair. After all, he was a frail old man. A few minutes later the dutiful Charles put the aged, inebriated man to bed as the grandfather clock chimed midnight.

Sunday morning arrived and the forgetful Earl didn't even think about the wooden box during the day. In fact he almost forgot about Sams impending dinner visit later that evening, until Charles reminded him half an hour before Sam was due to arrive.

Sam was very keen to meet grandad as Harry had told him last night that he didn't get chance to steal the cross. However, he knew that they were both happy to tell lies to get what they wanted so he wasn't sure whether to believe his brother or not. Did Harry actually steal it? Anyhow, he had the chance tonight to open the box, take a look, and find out if Harry was telling the truth.

While they had drinks Sam and the Earl chatted about the will. The conversation went well, but of course Sam was more interested in the wooden box at the other side of the room. Charles the butler soon entered the room and surprisingly decided to tidy the cushions on the settee at the far end of the room next to the table upon where the wooden box was. He took an unusually long time to do this, and Sam couldn't watch him for long as he was facing his grandad while he was talking through the contents of the will. The butler eventually left the room to prepare dinner but soon came back to tell the Earl that he had a phone call. To receive the call in the lobby the Earl left Sam alone in the lounge. This gave Sam the chance to open the box, which he did quickly and easily, but there was no cross inside, just a note that said "too late". He didn't appreciate this practical joke and was dismayed with his brother and would deal with him when he got back home.

A few minutes after Sam left the abbey for home Charles entered the lounge and gave the Earl his final whisky of the evening. Charles then wondered over in the direction of the wooden box and hovered over it with his back to the Earl. The Earl smiled at Charles and told him that he was too suspicious of the boys for his own good. However, when Charles opened the box he showed the Earl the note and also an empty box. The Earl was shocked and dumbstruck. He told Charles that he couldn't believe what one of the boys had done and that he was very upset, especially as he wasn't even sure which one of the boys was the thief. Charles smirked to himself as he did not like either of the boys. The Earl asked the butler to call the police so they could decide who took the cross from whatever fingerprints they would find.

The next day the police came to the abbey, completed some tests and then told both the Earl and Charles that there was only one set of fingerprints on the box, which belonged to Sam. The Earl was very upset with Sam and the police advised that they would visit the boys at their cottage within the next twenty four hours.

It is now late that evening and Sam is in his bed at the cottage. He was too upset with Harry when he arrived home and so went straight to bed. He had refused to speak to Harry at all as he was convinced that Harry had taken the cross and he would probably gloat about winning the bet with Sam. Both boys know that the police are on their way now to talk to them. While in bed Sam tries to think over in his mind how the cross had been taken and what actually happened before he opened the box on Sunday night to find only the note. Now he suddenly remembers that the butler was tidying up those cushions while Grandad talked about the will, so he reckons that Harry was telling the truth and it was probably the butler that took the cross and in doing so he would have set Sam up to get the blame knowing that Sam would probably leave fingerprints if he went for the cross. Sam had forgotten about the notion of fingerprints, and that the butler always wears white gloves. He is now sure that it must have been the butler who left the note for Sam in the box to make him think that Harry took it the night before, which was clever of him. He also feels bad about blaming Harry and wonders how he can get the butler back for setting him up. Sam grunts to himself; it was only last week that he had read an Agatha Christie book where "the butler did it".

While Sam is thinking this, Charles is in his own bedroom upstairs in the abbey. He is drinking his hot chocolate with a smile on his face. He dislikes the boys and reckons Sam is in serious trouble now as the fingerprints will point to him. It would have been easy for Charles to have set up either of the boys. He knows the code for the box, he knew the two boys would be here this week for supper and he also knew that temptation would mean that least one of them would try to open the box and leave fingerprints. After all they are not as smart as he is, and Charles knows this. It would have been simple for him to set one of the boys up. However, Charles would never let the cross be stolen as he respects the Earl and he knows that the Earl would have been miserable if either of his grandchildren got into trouble with the police.

Harry is also in his own bedroom with a smile on his face. He took gloves on Saturday evening as it was snowing. He used the gloves while opening the box to take the cross so there would be no fingerprints left from him. He knew Sam would try to open the box and he also knew that Sam wouldn't think to use gloves, so the only fingerprints on the box would be Sam's. He would be the one to get into trouble.

Harry removes the cross from his pocket and hides it in his room. When the police come it will be Sam who they will want to talk to and not him.

Short Story 5: Sights and Sounds

Theo is a normal, everyday single, thirty-year-old guy. He is a bit of a looker to the ladies, but hasn't had a girlfriend for a few months now. He does have a bachelor pad though and is now on the way to the shops for the weekly stocking of his fridge. His everyday life isn't usually very exciting, but the next few days will change his life.

On his way to the shops he witnesses a car crash, but the man who causes the crash drives off and leaves the scene. Theo is a good citizen so rushes to the other car, which has flipped over onto its roof. He thinks that the driver is the only one who is in the car, so he goes to her rescue. However, the roof of the overturned car is all bent and is now at ground level, so it is hard to see through the windows. At the driver's side he sees an arm squeezing out of the open window but can't see the driver as the distorted roof covers the driver from view.

The lady in the car struggles to speak and whispers the word "help" with a croaky voice through the metal, which makes her sound like a man. Theo now knows that she is alive and tells her not to speak but to breath regularly to save energy. Theo holds her hand and she squeezes his hand tight. He knows this means "please don't leave me". He continues to hold her hand and talks to her calmly to help her relax while waiting for the ambulance. Theo doesn't know it but she can feel her legs and arms so despite the crumbled roof, she is relatively okay. They can't see each other, in fact all Theo can see is her arm peering out of the window so he continues to hold her hand and talks to her through the body of the car to keep her calm.

The fire brigade and ambulance arrives and takes over

expertly. They take a long time to get her out so they tell Theo to go home while they are working out how to do it. They eventually get her out of the car, assess that she is okay and takes her to hospital for a checkup.

While at home Theo gets a call from the hospital and is told that the lady has cuts and bruises but will be okay. Amazingly, the only injury incurred was cuts to the face with four stitches to her right forearm. The lady has asked the ambulance man to thank Theo for being with her and making her comfortable and is sorry not to have seen him in person to thank him. She has called him her "whispering rescuer" as she never actually saw him, and will always think of him when she looks at her four stitch marks on her arm.

Now that Theo is at home he prepares for next weeks interview. He is out of work and the forthcoming interview appears promising as the job seems to him to be perfect. His good citizen act earlier in the day can be quoted if he gets asked questions about how he has helped others in the past.

A week later Theo drives to his interview. The company have a big swanky office in town. The interview with Tim, who is the boss, goes well. He tells Theo that he is the lead candidate and so will be asked to go to the second interview the following week where he will be interviewed this time by the hiring manager.

Theo is convinced that he will get the job now and is excited by the possibility of a new well-paid job. All he has to do is pass the second interview next week.

With the stress of a job interview removed Theo can now focus on getting a date with someone. Despite his good looks he hasn't had much success with the ladies over the last few months. However he has recently seen a description of a lovely girl on his new dating app. She has an English degree, as does he, and her profile is perfect. She has even given him a tick on the app, which means she likes his profile. They haven't seen a picture of each other yet but looks don't matter to him, it's the person inside that counts, and hopefully they will meet soon.

After many weeks of exchanging texts Theo and his online date feel comfortable to meet. His date suggests a meet in his local pub on 2nd May at 3pm for lunch. That's great for Theo, he likes this pub as it serves good food and has a nice feel to it. Then Theo remembers that the second interview for the job is at 1pm on the same day as his date. Fortunately, the pub is only a short drive from the company so if he is lucky then the timings could work out and he can do both on the same day.

At last the day arrives for both the second interview at 1pm and the date at 3pm.

Theo prepares for the interview in the morning, dresses smartly and gets to the interview in good time and is asked to wait in reception while Susan, the hiring manager, is called.

While siting waiting in reception for the hiring manager he thinks about the date he has with the girl from the dating app later in the afternoon. He finally got a picture of her yesterday, so now he knows what she looks like and he also got some more general information about her. She drives a black BMW and has a career job locally. But now that makes Theo think. As he arrived for the interview a few minutes ago he saw a few BMW cars in the car park adjacent to the company building, and one of them is black.

His thoughts are suddenly interrupted by the receptionist who tells him that Susan is ready to interview him. Theo goes cold as he remembers that Sue was also the name of the girl who he is dating at 3pm. While walking to the interview room his mind juggles all the information he has just gathered. Are his interviewer and his later romantic date the same person? He is also a bit concerned because he is now late for the interview, but it's not his fault as he was kept for twenty minutes in the waiting room.

They get to the room and the pleasant reception lady tells Theo to take a seat in the interview room and Susan, the hiring manager will be along soon.

Theo, now alone in the room waits for his interviewer and takes a seat in the room. As he does so he sees a certificate on the wall celebrating Sue's BA Honours in English and his stomach turns cold again. His online date has an English degree as well.

A few seconds later the door is opened and a lady walks in while listening to her iPhone. Her head is bent into her shoulder intently listening to the call such that Theo can't see her face well. She doesn't pay him much attention as she is engrossed in the call. Theo can hear the man on the other end of the phone giving her a hard time and talking so fast the lady hasn't got a chance to say anything to defend herself. As she quietly walks from the door towards Theo with phone-to-ear she faintly mouths the word "sorry" to Theo, apologising for the call. She is careful that the man on the phone can't hear her, and puts her hand up to Theo in apology as she now walks to the desk and sits down. Now he can see her face as she eventually ends the call. Theo is stunned.

She isn't his online date but she is very, very attractive. They look at each other as he leans over the desk to shake hands with her, and the lady starts the conversation by introducing herself as Susan and before Theo can even say "hello" she describes the process of the interview and some detail about the job. She talks very quickly in a business-like fashion and obviously hasn't got time to waste.

At last Theo gets a chance to say something and thanks Sue for giving him the opportunity of being interviewed for the job. As Theo gets to the end of this opening sentence, he notices Sue's face turn white. Theo asks if she is feeling well and as he does this he notices four stitches on her right forearm.

Susan isn't his 3pm internet date. She has turned white as she is the lady who had the car crash last week. Not only has she just heard her "whispering rescuer" again but she has now seen him for the first time.

Short Story 6: A Bridge Between Life and Death

On a miserable wintry December evening Sally has just finished work for the day in central London. She is now walking towards London Bridge on her way to the station on this dark, cold evening. Her smart phone has been switched off for most of the day so that no one could hassle her, but now she turns it on and watches it load up the emails that she has missed during the day. She is adept at simultaneously walking and reading texts. Sally is very used to this walk as she does it every weekday and still enjoys the views across London every night. Now, as she approaches the start of the bridge she feels the chill of the cold and takes in the view of the big brightly lit buildings. However, the main view that she will get tonight won't be much fun at all.

The walk to waterloo station is one that many people do as a routine and Sally recognises a few of the people that she regularly sees on this daily commute back to the station. Just in front of her is the middle aged, slightly balding guy who usually gives her a smile when they see each other. They had briefly spoken once a few days ago, and he had introduced himself as Steve. Sally knows little about Steve other than he is single, works for Mencap and looks after a youngster occasionally, who is autistic. So, as far as she is concerned he seems a decent bloke.

Steve has just joined the group of people crossing the bridge and is only a meter or so in front of Sally as they both start to cross the bridge in the dark, with only the lights of the bridge for guidance.

Sally can tell that pretty much everyone on the walk

back to the station has just come out of work. Their lanyards dangling from their neck gives them away. She had seen Steve's lanyard a few days ago and quickly read that he worked for Mencap, an agency supporting people with learning disabilities. She guessed he was a people type person as he looks that sort. Her own lanyard is ancient now, simply bearing her tired photo and a brief statement of her job as Marketing Director of a clothes company.

Tonight, the chill has started to bite and Sally has noticed this acutely as she has forgotten her scarf. As she fastens the zip on her coat both she and Steve start to cross Waterloo bridge in the cold. She looks to her right across the river and notices the wonderful London lights. As she does this, she hears a commotion in front of her at the middle of the bridge. Something is happening further on from the group of people in front of her and she can't work out what is going on. Then, as she continues walking across the bridge she sees someone standing on the ledge of the bridge wall. It is a young girl, who is now shouting out loud to everyone. Then Sally realises that she is a jumper.

It has been all too common recently to hear about people attempting to commit suicide by jumping from a bridge. This poor young girl has decided that today it is her turn. She is clearly in a high state of agitation and Sally thinks she must have had some kind of mental health breakdown.

The young girl is now screaming to whoever cares to listen to her as they walk past, but the public who are walking across the bridge are all quickly trying to disappear. They don't want to get involved. The rush of people in front of Sally to get past the girl and to the other end of the bridge now leaves a void between these people and Sally, who is still walking close to Steve. They are both now next to the girl with seemingly no-one else around. Suddenly it seems that is just the three of them there.

The girl screams again and Steve stops instantly and as Sally is right behind him, she stops as well. The two of them are now only a couple of meters away from the girl on the ledge. The young girl can see them both so continues to scream, but this time directly at Sally and Steve.

Sally is flummoxed. She doesn't know what to do, but then Steve starts to talk to the girl. Sally is relieved as she wouldn't have the slightest clue what to say and decides to stand where she is and at least support Steve with her presence. Everyone else seems to have scarpered.

Steve has a calm voice and asks the girl to relax and have a conversation with him.

Of course, thinks Sally, Steve works for Mencap, so he will know what to do as he is probably used to dealing with people who have mental health issues. Sally continues to listen to Steve talking to the girl in a calm, relaxed way, despite the freezing, biting wind.

While Steve is talking to the girl in a soothing voice Sally looks around. She knows this bridge well. If the girl does jump she will not hit the water but instead will land on the concrete that is supporting the bridge pillar, which means that she will instantly be killed, which is probably why she chose that particular part of the bridge to jump. Sally also notices that the public standing behind both Steve and her have stopped a discreet ten meters or so, to give Steve some space to work his verbal magic with the young girl. A policeman has now made his way to the front of them and after assessing the situation has called for support on his radio, to help assist the girl. However, everyone on the bridge knows that it will take time for help to come and the next few minutes are critical for Steve to encourage the young girl to come down, or at least keep her calm until further help arrives.

Sally realises that she is now standing closer to Steve than ever before and feels his comforting presence, while his lanyard is waving about in the breeze. She has really warmed to him now as she looks at his photo, which shows his engaging smile. While Steve continues his comforting words to the girl Sally is relived that it is he who has taken control of the situation and not her. She would say entirely the wrong thing.

Steve asks the girl to come down and have a chat with him, but the girl responds by screaming at him about how rubbish her life is and that she has had enough of everything. The girl then looks at Sally is if to ask for help, so Sally reinforces Steve's request for her to come down. However, the girl then gives Sally a volley of verbal abuse, which frightens her. Then, Steve puts his hand up and asks the girl to keep calm. He then tells the girl that he has a daughter of her age, that she also has mental health problems, and that she is receiving specialist help. This is all communicated by Steve in a slow methodical voice. Steve offers to connect the girl with the relevant people who can help her and he mentions that he works for Mencap. Sally is relieved that he is starting to calm her down and the girl seems to be responding to the comment about his daughter.

Steve then mentions to the girl that his daughter has a Bipolar Disorder condition and as soon as the girl hears this term she focusses acutely on Steve's eyes, so Sally suspects that the girl may also have this condition. Her thought is confirmed when the girl quitely asks the man a series of questions about his daughter, at which point Steve responds calmly with encouraging comments. Sally realises that he is again calming the girl down and is starting to gain her trust. He is also getting her to talk to him in a relaxed manner and it seems that she has lost the desire to shout now.

Sally looks at Steve with admiration and wonders what kind of training he must have had from Mencap to do this. What a stroke of luck that it is Steve who is here and not Sally's brother, who is a boxing instructor. He would have shouted back at the girl and goodness knows what the result of that would have been.

While Steve and the young girl exchange further words he mentions a technique that he uses at work when people get stressed or agitated, which is to breath in deeply and then breathe out over a ten second period. Steve tells her that this helps the body physically relax and asks her if they can both try this technique together. To Sally's surprise the young girl agrees. The crowd who are gathered behind them breathe a sigh of relief as this will take time and hopefully more medical staff will arrive soon to help.

Over the next few minutes they perform the exercise. Sally is immensely proud of Steve now as he is getting a great response from the girl, and so she whispers "well done" to Steve. Sally herself is falling for Steve's manner, charm and skill. Steve then asks the girl when was the last time that she went to the beach. They then both talk about the seaside and Steve reflects to her about how peaceful an empty, sandy beach is with its slow ripples of water at the shore. Sally inwardly smiles as she herself is feeling relaxed by Steve's clever words now. Steve ends with a request for the girl to come and get some coffee with him at the coffee shop at the end of the bridge. He extends his hand to her as an invite.

The crowd who have gathered behind the two of them now gasp as the young girl agrees to the request, takes Steve's hand, and comes down. They give Steve a rousing round of applause. Sally is really impressed with Steve but is shaking now that her adrenaline rush has stopped. She now needs a hot drink herself.

The policeman takes over the situation and the girl is given some aid by a recently arrived ambulance crew. They will take her to the hospital and Steve has offered to honour his promise of a coffee on another day, which the girl agrees to.

Ten minutes later Steve and Sally are in the coffee shop at the end of the bridge. Sally has offered to buy them both a hot drink and something to eat, for which Steve gratefully accepts.

As they sit in the coffee shop their food arrives and Sally looks at Steve. As she does this she again notices how charming he really is. He has a lovely natural manner which suits her style. She has already seen from his lanyard that he is single and of course, so is she. Sally hopes that there might be more to this coffee rendezvous than originally anticipated.

While drinking coffee Sally looks at Steve again in

admiration and tells him how proud she is of him for talking the girl down. She tells him how impressed she is and comments on how cleverly he used his professional skills and also his own daughter's medical condition to help him calm the girl and eventually get her down to safety. She asks Steve what kind of special training he received from Mencap to do what he did tonight.

Steve looks at Sally with a furrowed brow now and tells her that she is right, he does work at Mencap, but only as a computer assistant so he has no mental health training as such. He adds that he lied to the girl and doesn't have a daughter, but he did see a film where the lead character used his daughter's medical condition and breathing techniques and to calm a bridge jumper down. All Steve did was use common sense to talk her down.

Sally is shocked. She thought Steve was an expert at dealing with stressful situations and has misinterpreted completely what has happened, but she is still glad that this event led to them having coffee. She has fallen for his kindly manner, charm and skill. Well, kindly manner and charm at least. Two out of three isn't bad. Thank goodness some people can think quickly, she muses.

Short Story 7: The Lone Youngster on the Boundary

So, what can I say about myself? I am ten years old and I am currently watching Steve play cricket for the men's team at my local village cricket club in London, on a nice warm sunny day. It's an all-male event (and that includes me).

Steve loves his cricket. As well as this local club he also plays for his Mencap works cricket team. He is a superstar here as a few months ago he saved a girl from jumping off a bridge in London.

Steve adopted me when I came into this world ten years ago and he takes me with him to cricket as he knows I like to be with him. I watch Steve play cricket every Saturday afternoon. If it's a nice hot day I lie down on the grass by the boundary and watch him. Only him mind, I am not interested in the other people. If it is a cold day I can sit by the pavilion to keep warm, out of the wind.

I am only ten years old and the cricket club love having me there. The colts cricket team (under 12's) are practicing in the nets today. I'd love to grab one of those cricket balls and show them what I could do with it, but I shouldn't really.

Sometimes, my friends Bob and Dan (who are even younger than me) appear while I am watching Steve and we have fun playing games on the boundary. Bob and Dan prefer playing with themselves rather than with me, but when the three of us do play we have fun playing "tag". Mind you we do get told-off if we go over that cricket boundary rope.

Last Saturday was a hot day watching the cricket and I saw Judy on the other side of the boundary. She was with her mom and someone else. Wow, I really like Judy and I've seen her a few times before in our local kids park. But today she ignores me when they walk past. I am used to that. There is something about me that makes people ignore me but I am happy being on my own. I also occasionally have trouble understanding what people say, perhaps that's why people only briefly talk to me.

I do sometimes get company from the other players in Steve's team, while they are waiting to bat, but usually they ignore me. I think that's probably because I do get a bit excitable.

I have been ill recently but when it is sunny, like today, then I feel much better. Generally, people are a bit wary of me as I tend to stare at them but it doesn't bother me. They sometimes come up to me and then tease me as the patch over my right eye intrigues them slightly. They sometimes say "Hey patchy" and then they all laugh. I don't really mind.

Watching Steve is great. I am allowed a drink but for some reason the posh cricket club only let me drink water. If I get bored I just play with my teddy. He is a bit bedraggled now as I don't look after him well, but I like him. The players tease me by taking teddy off me, but he is mine so I try to get him back, which makes people laugh at me. The adults think it is fun to tease me.

Steve seems to be enjoying playing today, perhaps he is playing well, I don't really understand cricket so I don't know. I don't get why all those people are running around, mind you I hope the ball comes my way, then I can join in with them and give it back to that nice fielder who keeps saying "hi" to me as he walks past.

People only briefly talk to me but we all enjoy having tea and I look forward to that. The cricket team seem to have their own tea while the other people around have theirs sitting by the boundary. The tea break is a nice time but Steve won't let me have any of his sandwiches. Still, I do get something to eat which is fun, especially if Bob and Dan are nearby.

The cricketers are the only people who can go inside the pavilion. I wouldn't want to go in anyway, it's a bit scary in the dark pavilion. If I need a pee I tend to find a nearby tree round the back, I even had a "number two" once while no one was looking so don't tell anyone! It's great being round the back of the pavilion as it gives me a chance to have a look to see who is around to play with.

It is late in the day now and the game has finished on this hot day. A sweaty Steve is walking off the field with the other cricketers. The other player's wives and children go up to them and give them a hug. I follow them and find Steve. He gives me a cuddle. I watch Judy, Bob and Dan get into the boot of their cars while Steve puts my dog lead on me, retrieves my water bowl and picks up the poo I left by the tree. He also picks up teddy which I have almost shredded now. He gives me a toy bone and I jump in the car to go home.

In the car Steve turns and looks at me curled up in the back. He says something to me that I can't understand and then smiles at the jet black furry area over my right eye. The rest of my fur is white.

That's why I am called "Patch".

Short Story 8: The Perfect Steal

It is hard to imagine how to steal something without someone realising it. It can be difficult to do, but when you know how, you can surprise even your closest friend.

Mac and Neil are brothers who live together in a flat in the north of England. They are both in their late twenties and get on well but couldn't be more different from each other in personality.

Mac is the more adventurous of the two, and always has been. When he left school he was determined to go into the army and did well there. He is tall with broad shoulders and very athletic. Two tours of Afghanistan with the army taught him many extreme survival skills including keeping warm in snow, sleeping without being found by the enemy, finding scarce food in the hills and many other survival skills for a soldier to stay alive. He retired from the army on medical grounds recently and went to the north of England where his brother Neil let him stay in his flat while he got back on his feet.

Neil, however is more reserved, keeping himself to himself. The thought of being in the army would make him shiver. He did well academically at school and got a hatful of qualifications. He is now an I.T. consultant, well paid and has recently bought a flat. When at home he prefers to do introverted hobbies such as computer gaming rather than socialising with people, but he does keep in contact with his old school friends.

Now that Mac has returned from the army Neil is keen to help him reconnect with their old school friends and as it is now September it will soon be Franks birthday, their favourite old school buddy, and Frank always has a party.

These parties are legendary, where Frank invites twenty or so old school pals to his house for an evening's booze up. Franks female friends are invited as well but they tend not to come as they prefer to let the boys "do what boys do". It's an excuse for excessive eating, loud music and drinking till the small hours. All the lads know each other so although it's a raucous event nothing scandalous really happens. Frank even lets the next-door neighbours know about the party so that they can make alternative arrangements to avoid the noise. He doesn't know that this year his party will end up with a very strange ending.

The day of Frank's party arrives. It is a Saturday night and Mac and Neil make their way there with some serious quantities of booze, after visiting the local superstore.

Frank has a typical, standard three bed semi-detached house which he bought a few years ago. It's the same design as Neil's house up the road, and pretty much everybody's house in the area. Frank loves his house because it is simple, basic but well designed. Upstairs has a bathroom, a landing with three bedrooms and a loft, while downstairs there is a decent sized kitchen, toilet and a living room which is open plan with a conservatory. This is where Frank works during the day. All very standard really. The garden is small and manageable. He works at home and only has to go to his work office on the occasional weekday. The house is cheap and easy to maintain, the only expense he had to endure recently was to rectify a drain blockage a few months ago and then a week later he had to get someone in to eliminate some rats on the roof. He had to get that sorted swiftly of course. The rats came back recently but hopefully the second visit from the rodent expert has done the trick.

Frank is at home and is prepared for his twenty or so mates to come and enjoy the food and booze which will dominate the evening. They have attended his parties for the last ten years, so they all know the format of the night and as he pours himself a drink he can see Mac and Neil arrive. Its not long before they are all there and start to enjoy the evening.

The evening goes well. Much food is eaten and vast quantities of booze is drunk, so the upstairs and downstairs toilets get many visits. There are also many drunken conversations that take place through the night, which get weirder as more booze is consumed over the course of the evening.

It's now nearly midnight and Frank laughs as he watches his friend Ben throwing some pizza out of the window at the crows. He misses them of course. Frank joins Mac in the living room and starts a conversation, and both of them slurs considerably to the other. Then the conversation turns slightly serious as Frank interrogates Mac on his Army days. Mac changes the subject as those days are painful and well over now. Neil comes over to join them both and the conversation inevitably gets to the subject of computer games on which both Neil and Frank have spent much money over the years.

Neil is suddenly reminded about Frank's recent acquisition. Frank is a stamp collector and has recently bought a small booklet containing some very old and valuable stamps. They are worth at least ten thousand pounds. Frank tells both brothers Neil and Mac that the booklet of stamps is kept in an unlocked desk drawer in the second bedroom, so Mac thinks that they will be easy to find.

Mac suggests to Frank that he should get the booklet insured as someone might steal it from what is a poorly secured house. Frank replies that both the front and back door are solid and well bolted. They are the only way into the house from the outside and the windows are all UPVC with locks. After all, Frank reminds them that he works for a security company so he knows how to secure his house. He tells Mac and Neil that he works at home during the day, so it's unlikely that anyone would get through the front or back door and then past him without him knowing.

Then suddenly, Mac lays down a challenge. He bets a thousand pounds that he can steal the booklet of stamps from Frank. It sounds to Frank like a drunken brag from Mac as they are all sozzled now, so Frank thinks he can get some easy money here as Mac looks very drunk and he accepts the challenge. Mac offers his hand to shake on the deal and says the booklet of stamps will be stolen by midnight tomorrow, which is Sunday. Frank agrees and shakes Mac's hand. That's less than twenty-four hours for Mac to do the steal. Neil is the witness of the bet and once they shake on it they move on and all three mingle with the other house guests, in their drunken stupor.

Mac privately tells his brother Neil how he will steal the booklet of stamps while Frank is working tomorrow, which is a Sunday. Frank has already moved on to talk to his old next-door neighbour who has arrived for a beer.

Time passes and Sunday morning arrives. Frank is now tidying up his house after the party. He has only had a few hours sleep and thinks back on the party. He had previously fallen asleep in a drunken stupor at one o'clock in the morning, which then became the end of the party. The lads made Frank comfortable on the settee. Then they left one by one while singing drunken football songs. Mark, Frank's best friend had also nodded off for a while and when he woke at 2am he realised that Frank was sleeping on the settee and on walking round the house he couldn't see anyone else left, inside so he carefully locked up and left his buddy asleep.

Frank had then woken at 8am with a massive hangover for a Sunday morning. He now feels better after some juice and tidies the flat as he has to work today. He doesn't like working on a Sunday but this week he needs to. As he finishes up the disposing of beer cans and stale food he remembers the bet where Mac said he would steal the booklet of stamps by midnight tonight. It is now 11 o'clock and it occurs to Frank that Mac has to get a move on to try and get into the house for the steal or he will miss the deadline for the steal.

He notices that the kitchen sink is blocked which isn't a surprise considering all the food last night. If that wasn't bad enough, in the quiet of the house he can hear faint scratching noises upstairs. "Rats again!" he shouts to himself. Why do problems always come at the same time, especially as he has to work now? He can fix the blocked sink quickly now but the rats will have to wait till tomorrow as he must start working soon or he will miss Wednesday's office deadline. He then decides not to fix the blockage yet but goes to the conservatory to start work at his desk.

While he is working in the conservatory he thinks about the bet while he chews the top of a pen. He if loses the bet then he is down a grand, so he'd better be sure that Mac can't get into the house. He is now in the conservatory which contains the back door so he can see if Mac decides to come around the back. The other external door, the front door, is secure and he has already checked that. So, there is no way Mac can get in. However, to be sure, he gets up and checks both doors yet again and also checks that all the windows are locked. He then walks round the house and in order checks the bathroom, all the other rooms upstairs and then the kitchen, living room and conservatory downstairs. He checks to see that everything is as usual. Even the downstairs toilet gets a check. He is sure that there is nothing unusual in any rooms, cupboards or closets that Frank could have left last night to help him break in today, that is if he manages to get through the impenetrable front door. He smiles to himself. There is no way Mac can get in!

Then he panics. Perhaps Mac already took the booklet last night while everyone was drunk. Frank checks that the booklet is still there in the upstairs bedroom. He breathes a sigh of relief as he sees it is still there. He smiles. All is well. Only a few hours to go.

He texts Mac to say good luck. Mac texts back telling him to watch his stamps disappear and to get his money ready. Frank smiles.

He goes back to work in the conservatory. The kitchen drain blockage now smells, and again he can hear that faint scratching noise upstairs. He reckons the rats on the roof are feeding on the pizza that his buddy Ben threw out of the window last night.

He works for another hour in the conservatory while enjoying some real coffee.

Then Frank sees a text from Mac on his phone to say he has stolen the stamps!

Frank can't believe it. How did he get in the house in the last hour when he checked all the rooms, doors and windows? It has only been half an hour or so since he last saw the booklet of stamps. Frank runs upstairs and sure enough the desk drawer is open and the booklet of stamps has been taken. He runs downstairs and gets to the front door and can see that no-one has got in from the outside. So, he couldn't have got in through the front door; and Frank was sitting next to the back door in the conservatory for the last half an hour, so how did he get in? Then Frank decides to check the only window large enough for an adult to enter, which is the landing window. He goes upstairs and stands on the hallway landing and looks around. There is nothing unusual in the bedrooms or the bathroom, and yes, the landing window is still locked. The house is secure.

While standing on the landing outside his bedroom his phone pings again. Mac is asking him when he wants to hand over the money. From the landing he senses the bad smell from the kitchen sink which has permeated upstairs now. He thinks about the smell as he looks into the bathroom from his position on the landing, but that can wait till tomorrow. Then he thinks to himself that he hasn't heard the rats making that scratching noise from the roof for a while. That makes him look above his head to where he thought the scratching came from. The loft hatch is slightly open.

Now Frank gets it.

The scratching noise wasn't rats. It was Mac. He never left the house last night after the party. Instead, he waited for all the drunken lads to start leaving the party then he used his army skills to quietly sneak upstairs and silently get into the loft. He then kept quiet while hiding in the loft for a few hours. He was used to sleeping rough and silently while on manoeuvres with the army, so a loft wouldn't be much trouble for him. The scratching noise was him opening and closing the loft hatch. He took the booklet from the bedroom then left through the front door, which can be opened from the inside but not the outside.

Mac lives in Neil's house, which is the same design as Frank's so he knows the house layout, in particular what the loft looks like and how to get in it.

Frank then hears the ping of his phone. It's a note from Mac.

"You forgot I was in the army. I slept in your loft last night. Open your front door."

Frank opens the front door and on the step is the booklet of stamps with a note from Mac which said

"Forget the money. Never make bets that you can't win!"

Frank smiles and closes the door.

Short Story 9: An Unlikely Witness

It is unusual for little old ladies to play a key part in a murder case but that's exactly what happened in a small country village in south England .

Mrs Sanders was a little old grey-haired lady who lived on the ground floor of a two story set of flats in a village located in the countryside of southern England. Her neighbours were of a quiet nature, except the man who lived directly above her. He was a particularly unpleasant man and Mrs Sanders impression of him didn't improve when she learned that he had some time ago been accused of murder. He had committed the crime but avoided jail on a technicality. She was very wary of him as he didn't seem to hide is "nastiness".

Fortunately, she didn't have any need to talk to him from day to day. Sometimes she passed him in the shared corridor of the flat, when he returned from his grocery shopping. At least she usually got a relatively polite greeting. One positive aspect of this man was that he had a very nice girlfriend who visited him frequently. However, her visits usually ended in big blazing rows which Mrs Sanders could hear, as the sound permeated through the floorboards to her flat. Mrs Sanders even feared for the girl's safety once or twice. The nasty man was known to carry a knife occasionally and he was also known to have a bad temper. This, alongside his past history, wasn't something pleasant to think about. The girl was very sweet though and every time she visited the nasty man she would knock at Mrs Sander's door and ask if she was okay. Occasionally she would bring her flowers. How nice of her, thought the little old lady. She couldn't work out how such a thoughtful lady would want to be with such a nasty man.

Living below this man was bad enough for Mrs Sanders but what was really annoying about him was that he wouldn't fix his noisy plumbing. He probably spent his money on booze and unhealthy food instead, thought Mrs Sanders. Every time he turned his taps on there was a loud squeak and when he had a shower the clanging was intolerable. It was that distinct clanging sound every time the shower was used that told her that he was having a shower, and it lasted for an annoying ten minutes or so. He obviously liked long showers. Mrs Sanders had to turn her radio up to counter the noise.

It was on a Friday afternoon when things really turned nasty. Little did Mrs Sanders know that she would be pivotal in deciding the future of this unpleasant man.

On this Friday Mrs Sanders was returning to her flat from her late afternoon grocery visit. She got to her front door and saw the man pass her to go upstairs to his flat. He was also carrying some groceries with two filet beef steaks sitting proudly on top. Looks like a good supper for him and his nice girlfriend, thought Mrs Sanders. The man seemed in good spirits at the time, but Mrs Sanders was suspicious of him, as usual.

She went into her flat and prepared some tea. At about 6pm she had a knock on the door. Of course, it was the nice girlfriend popping in to see if she was okay. She bought her flowers and this time she also brought some chocolates, the thought of which gave Mrs Sanders a glowing feeling inside. Mrs Sanders had a short but pleasant chat to the girl who said that she was going to end her relationship with the man tonight. As Mrs Sanders said goodnight and closed her door she was worried what that horrible man might do to the girl when he was given the news.

The little old lady prepared her tea. She then got ready to settle into her armchair in front of the warm cosy fire to do a spot of reading while the bitter wind raged and the rain poured down noisily outside the flat, on this stormy night. As she opened her book she could hear the squeak of the pipes as either the man or the nice girl turned the taps for presumably a hand wash or to do this dishes. At least it wasn't the loud clanging of the shower thought Mrs Sanders, and she put the radio on to listen to some soft music.

Then it happened.

A big thud. Not just a normal thud but a muffled one which to Mrs Sanders was clearly a body falling to the floor heavily. The old lady recognised this sound instinctively after what had happened in that flat a few years earlier. The previous owner of the horrible man's flat was a kindly old man who died from a heart attack. Mrs Sanders heard the thud of his body as he fell to the floor. Now, Mrs Sanders has heard that same thud sound of a body falling on the floor again. The thud was so loud that some of the other residents in the adjacent flats would have probably heard it as well. The little old lady knew that the girl was going to give him bad news, and that horrible man has a few kitchen knives in his flat for those steaks. It didn't take much for Mrs Sanders to put two and two together.

Mrs Sanders walked to her telephone to call the police. She dialled the 999 number and got an efficient sounding lady on the phone. But when she asked if Mrs Sanders wanted the ambulance or the police Mrs Sanders couldn't hear very well as the clanging noise in the upstairs flat started up. This infuriated Mrs Sanders as she was desperate to get her message across. When the emergency services lady repeated the question Mrs Sanders finally understood, and then asked for the police. After giving all the details she eventually finished the call and put the phone down, then locked her door, just in case.

Half an hour later there was a knock at her door. She hoped it wasn't the nasty man coming after her, but instead it was the police. They said that the girl had indeed been stabbed to death and they had come to take a statement from her. Had she seen anything? Would she make a statement? Mrs Sanders was very upset and all she could do to help was to say that she had had a short chat to the girl and that she had also later heard the thud of the body as it hit the floor. Mrs Sanders also told the police that the girl said she was going to end the relationship. The police told Mrs Sanders that they suspected that the man had stabbed her, but the man says that the girl committed suicide with the knife while he had a shower, and in their opinion the scene of the crime did look consistent with a suicide, although he could have set that up. The police were trying to keep an open mind and in the meantime they were getting as many statements as possible from the people who lived in this particular block of flats. They needed some witness statements to help build a case against the man, but at the moment they had nothing.

The police left Mrs Sanders and she got a drink of juice and went back to her armchair to recover from the shock. Mrs Sanders assembled her thoughts while resting in the armchair. So, the nasty man has killed that lovely girl with a kitchen knife and he seems to have got away with it by setting up a suicide scene. It must have been a messy business with all that blood. She needed to think if she had seen or heard anything that would help convict this horrible man.

Mrs Sanders needed a hot drink now. She went to the kitchen, turned the tap on and poured some water into the kettle. The tap made her think of the squeaking of the nasty man's upstairs taps and the annoying clanging of his shower and how that always infuriated her. At least that won't happen for a while, with the man taken away for questioning for a few days.

She then thought about the call to the emergency services. The lady who took her call must have thought she was a stupid deaf old lady as Mrs Sanders couldn't hear what was being said to her because of the clanging noise upstairs. She was in her nineties after all. It was when she had that thought that Mrs Sanders suddenly got it, and she smiled to herself.

She had found the way to nail that horrible man.

She sat back down again in her armchair and went the though evening events again in her mind to confirm to herself that she had got it right. It dawned on her that the clanging sound that she heard from the upstairs shower happened at exactly the same time that she was on the phone to the emergency services, which was a good minute or so after Mrs Sanders had heard the thud of the body hitting the floor. This means that the man had his shower after the girl died and not at the same time. So he was lying when he said to police that the girl committed suicide with the knife at the same time that he had a shower. The clanging was a minute or so after the thud of the body on the floor, and he wouldn't have had a shower after his girlfriend had just knifed herself. Instead, what must have happened was that he had had a shower after he had knifed her himself, presumably to wash the blood off him.

Mrs Sanders smiled again and called the police.

She was the witness and now she had him

Short Story 10: So Who Did it?

This is a story of a simple theft from a family home. The question was, who was the villain?

Mr and Mrs Hunter were a married couple in their mid-fifties. They had four children, Simon, Alice, Olive and Tucker. Simon lived at home with mum and dad but the two girls, Alice and Olive, had already fled the nest having bought a flat together at the other end of the village. The other child was Tucker who also didn't live at home anymore. He lived in a more sinister place.

Mr and Mrs Hunter lived with Simon in the family home, but they were not alone as they had a loud, snappy, terrier dog called Fluffy. Alice and Olive had already been thinking about moving into their own flat, then when Fluffy arrived to live with the Hunters a few months ago the dog was so noisy that they left home swiftly and bought the flat, just for a bit of peace. That left Simon living with his parents. Simon loved Fluffy, even though he yapped at the slightest disturbance or visitor. Mind you, a good bone and a walk everyday kept Fluffy happy.

Tucker was twenty-three and in jail. He was the black sheep of the family; a complete rebel having mixed with the wrong crowd, but was soon to be released from jail in June after a two-year stint there for theft and damage to property. When he went to jail the Hunters then moved house to the next village, to get away from whispering neighbours.

Mr Hunter himself was a keen ornithologist and so kept a range of expensive cameras and scopes. He wasn't a collector but could not help himself when new camera models became available. As such he had some very expensive equipment kept in his downstairs study. He was clumsy though. He had just bought the latest Nikon camera and was annoyed with himself for spilling some fluid on it that he used to clean the lenses. Unfortunately the fluid was a smelly, aromatic cleaning solvent which oozed into the soft fabric of the camera case making it stink. He had only had the new camera for a few weeks. This would now make it more difficult next year when he would probably sell it second hand and replace it with a new model. Fortunately, his expensive hobby was funded by his well-paid job as a banker.

Simon, the youngest of the four children was now eighteen and in the process of completing his A Levels. He had been in a few scrapes with friends but had never broken the law, didn't smoke, and only drank a little alcohol so Mr and Mrs Hunter weren't too worried about him. After all he was a bright spark and looking forward to getting to university, to study maths which would suit his academic strengths.

Alice and Olive had both done well for themselves. Both had gone into banking straight from school and now that they had bought their flat together they were both well set up to advance their careers and social life.

It is now summer time and as 2nd June approached Mrs Hunter became apprehensive as her son Tucker would be released from his two-year jail sentence on this day. She was concerned about his welfare. Would he be straight, or return back to crime? In her mind it all depended on who he would hang out with.

On the day of Tuckers release from jail Mrs Hunter got herself ready to pick him up. She got to jail in good time and Tucker appeared fine. He was in good spirits and spoke well in the car about how he wanted to stop stealing things, make amends and get on with his life. However, Mrs Hunter new Tucker could spin a good story so wasn't sure how much of this to believe. Mum told Tucker of dad's recent expensive camera purchases, which put a smile on Tuckers face.

Tucker was keen to see the new family home as he had been in jail when the Hunters moved house after he had been locked up. She took him straight home and Tucker had lunch with both mum and dad, where they caught up on the two-year gap. Tucker would then stay with Alice and Olive in their flat for a couple of days while he got sorted.

While the three of them were having lunch Simon arrived home from a visit to the gym. Tucker and Simon greeted each other heartily. Tucker suggested that they go to the pub that evening to celebrate his return.

So that evening, the day before the theft, Tucker took Simon to the Feathers pub, which was over the road from their new family home. Simon was surprised that Tucker not only wanted to go to the untidy pub over the road, but then sit and drink outside on the bench which had a view of their house. He was surprised because their favourite pub was a short walk away and they both knew it served better beer. However, the boys did sit outside the Feathers pub and had a few drinks while they caught up on the gossip. While sitting outside, Simon was aware of Tucker looking over Simon's shoulder occasionally. He looked to see where Tucker was looking but he wasn't sure if he was looking at the good-looking girl on the pavement, or mum and dad's family home. Anyway, as far as Simon was concerned Tucker was back home now and cracking some great jokes which made him smile. After a good few beers Simon returned home and Tucker said he would make his way back to the girls flat.

The next evening was the night of the theft. Mr and Mrs Tucker had gone to bed after having a few whiskies with Simon, who was drinking some soda. They asked Simon to lock up before he went to bed.

In the morning Mr Hunter got up with a heavy head, to find that many of his cameras and scopes had been stolen and his study was a mess. About ten thousand pounds worth of equipment had gone. He was devastated. He mumbled to himself that Tucker had only been out of jail for a day and now this has happened.

Mrs Hunter and Simon came downstairs and joined in the search. Simon then said he was going in his car to Alice and Olives flat to tell them the news.

When Simon left, Mr Hunter called the police, who came and assessed the situation. Mr and Mrs Hunter were interviewed, and statements were taken. Simon then returned from his trip in the car, gave the police a statement and told the police that he thought that he had locked up last night, but now can't remember if he did it or not.

The front door had not been damaged and Mr Hunter had found it open when he came downstairs in the morning. The police concluded that as there was no damage to the door then someone who had a key must have entered and taken the items. Mrs Hunter wept slightly as she remembered yesterday while talking to Simon she giving Tucker a key so he could live with them again after he had spent a few days with Alice and Olive. She told the police this. Simon also mentioned to the police that Tucker had suggested having a drink over the road the evening before and to sit outside when it was cold. He also said that he caught Tucker looking over his shoulder at the house, probably to figure out how to enter the property as it was new to him.

The police agreed that as nobody outside the family had a key then it was probably a family member who did this and the officers left to interview Tucker and also Alice and Olive at their flat, as each of them had a key to the Hunters house. They said that they would probably arrest Tucker depending on what he said. Mrs Hunter went to her room and wept.

When the police returned to the Hunters house later that day they asked to speak to Mr and Mrs Hunter and Simon.

The police told them that they had suggested to Tucker that it was a coincidence that the theft had been made just a day after his release. They also put it to Tucker that he had received a key to the house from mum and that he had worked out how to get access to the house while having an evening drink with Simon. However, the police also said that they were then told by Alice that Tucker couldn't have committed the crime as by nine o'clock he was so drunk on brandy at their flat they had to call the doctor, as he lay on the settee "drunk as a skunk".

The police then looked at Mr Hunter and asked the big question, which was about the dog. They asked if there was any sound from Fluffy that evening. When the police arrived earlier in the morning Fluffy had been taken for a walk by a next-door neighbour so the police didn't realise that the Hunters even had a dog. The Hunters replied that Fluffy hadn't made a sound during the night, which was strange as Fluffy is very nervous and the slightest sound of a house break would have set him off.

They all then looked at Simon. Simon was in the house that night and Fluffy was used to him being there so the dog wouldn't make a sound at him even if he came in or out of the front door.

Then it came to Mr Hunter. Simon had unexpectedly offered him and mum some whisky that evening, presumably now to encourage a deep sleep for them. It was also strange that Simon went in his car to Alice and Olives house in the morning to tell them the news. Why didn't he just use his mobile? He must have put the stolen items in his car boot the night before and then took them to whoever he was selling them to the following morning, when he said he was going to the girls flat.

Mr Hunter looked at Simon and accused him of stealing his gear and framing Tucker. Simon denied it, of course. He had taken the gear but knew that no one could prove it.

Mr Hunter decided there was only one way to sort this. He asked the police to open Simon's car boot. Simon thought he was safe as he had got rid of the gear earlier in the day, but he opened his boot all the same.

Mr Hunter then smirked as he leant into the boot and sniffed. On the floor of the boot he could smell aromatic solvent that had come from his camera case. One of the stolen items was his new camera which had aromatic solvent soaked into the carrier case, which must have rubbed against the car boot floor. A tell-tale sign to Mr Hunter that Simon had taken his camera. He looked accusingly at Simon.

Simon eventually confessed to the crime and was taken to the station by the police.

Mr Hunter looked at his wife sorrowfully…..another offspring to go to jail.

Short Story 11: Tools of the Trade

Thefts from garden centres are not uncommon. In this case though, it is not so much about who is doing it but how.

Tom has been working in his local garden centre for a year now. He has progressed well and the staff have started to warm to him. They were wary of him when he first started because they knew he had spent time in the regional Young Offenders Prison for burglary related crimes. As time went on however, the garden centre staff were impressed by Tom's commitment to the job and his engaging personality. It seemed to the staff that the company's policy of giving offenders a second chance was proving successful. However, Tom was tempted to regress back to his bad ways, so the question was, would his new-found morals prevent him from returning to crime?

Now in his mid-twenties Tom has both a flat and this regular job, so has become quite independent of his family. He is sharp, quick witted and picks new ideas up quickly. Some of these traits in the past had led ultimately to his prison sentence, but nowadays the garden centre benefits from his smartness.

The garden centre is a basic, functional shop selling all forms of garden equipment. Wheelbarrows, lawnmowers, spades, forks, and compost are all sold there as well as other typical garden centre items. One of the garden centre's innovations was to sell sand, not in bags but loose. The adjacent forest which the garden centre owns has plenty of sand underground, which the company harvests occasionally to provide the sand to sell commercially. Customers would ask for either five or ten kilos of sand and Tom would use a wheelbarrow to take the loose sand from the site to the car park, where both staff and customers have parked their cars. Tom would then unload the sand into the boot of the customer's car, where the customer had provided their own tub to take the sand away. This innovation avoided using plastic packaging, which was good for the planet, in terms of being sustainable. In fact, Tom's main role has now revolved around coordinating the transfer of sand to the customer's car as this purchase is so popular. He usually uses a showroom wheelbarrow to transport the sand. By doing this, the customers get their sand to their car and are also tempted to buy the showroom wheelbarrow as well, which occasionally happens. At £50 a barrow, this idea is good business for the company, as well as selling the sand itself.

It was in the summer when Tom noticed something strange occurring. As he was taking yet another barrowful of sand to a customer's car he noticed someone on site that he had seen on a number of occasions previously. He watched this time as he saw this person enter the garden centre again. Tom stopped what he was doing and stared at the person. It was then that he realised that the person he had seen was Geoff. Geoff used to work at the garden centre some months ago but left suspiciously and without reason, as far as the he and the other staff were concerned. Tom didn't recognise him because now he was sporting a new beard, a hoody and a shifty cap. Geoff was clearly trying to be disguised. Tom also realised that although he had seen Geoff arrive recently on a number of occasions, he had never consciously realised who it really was. He now also remembers that he had never actually seen him use the customer exit.

So, Tom completed his immediate task of taking the sand to the customer's car and then he went to find Geoff. What he found was revealing.

Following Geoff from a distance Tom saw exactly what he was up to. Geoff would walk in to the building via the public entrance. None of the staff recognised him as they were so busy, and Geoff's disguise was just about good enough. Geoff would then pick up some shop items and then, when he was sure no-one could see, he would steal them by walking through the locked door of the staff exit. He still had the keypad code for the staff door from the time when he used to work at the Garden Centre, and that meant that he could leave without being noticed. He could also avoid the product scanners while secretly exiting the building. Once outside he would then get into his transit van for his escape. His van was big enough for any of the tools and garden equipment that he could steal. The garden centre had CCTV but none of them were by the staff exit and car park. Geoff knew he was therefore safe and could get away with the steal.

Before Tom has a chance to tell his boss what he has seen it is time to close the centre as it is now 5pm. The manager then calls all the staff together as soon as the public have left and then makes an announcement to the staff. He reveals to them that over the last few months the stock taking report is showing that items from the store are being stolen. Forks, spades, trowels, wheelbarrows and compost have been taken, although they don't yet have details on how many units of each have been taken. Tom now reveals to the team that he has seen Geoff and suspects that he has been seen stealing things. The staff are shocked that a previous employee has not only been in the building unnoticed but is also stealing from them. Today's CCTV showed them that Geoff had been hovering suspiciously over some small tools and then stealing them. They can now understand how Geoff managed to smuggle small items to his transit van but they can't figure out how he managed to get big items past them and to his van unnoticed.

The manager calls the police and Geoff is arrested. Of course, the stolen items have long gone but at least Geoff is now behind bars.

Even though Geoff has been caught, the manager is sure that Tom is also stealing some products as well as Geoff. He is convinced that Tom has hidden some small tools in the barrows of sand that he takes to customers' cars. He thinks that after Tom takes the sand to the customer's car and the customer leaves the site Tom then takes the small tools he had hidden within the sand in the wheelbarrow and takes them to his own car. The manager is sure that is how the small tools are being taken from the centre. Sue, one of the cashiers had in the past seen Tom take a barrow of sand to customers' cars on many occasions and sometimes she noticed that Tom appeared suspiciously cagey, which meant to her that he was up to no good. She now tells the manager that she is sure that buried in the sand of the barrow are hidden some small store items. Sue has in the past caught young members of staff stealing sweets in their pockets. She noticed their suspicious body language at the tills, so the manager trusts Sue's instincts. The manager also knows that although Geoff has stolen from the store and is behind bars now, his stolen items didn't account for absolutely all the missing stock items, so he was convinced that Tom was also stealing as well, even if it is only a small trowel or two, hidden in the sand of the barrow.

Sure enough, Tom is indeed stealing from the store, but what and how? The manager needs to catch him out but does not know how. He has completed a number of previous spot checks on Tom over the last few weeks but when he has checked deep beneath the sand in the barrow (as Tom takes it to the customers car) he finds nothing. Even when Sue gives the manager the nod that Tom appears suspicious, he immediately runs up to Tom and checks the sand in the barrow, but there is nothing hidden there. He can never catch him out and he just can't work out how he has hidden and stolen stock and never been found out.

It is now 5.30pm at the end of the week and Tom is on his way home to his flat after a hard days work. He drives back home in his car pleased with himself that he has stolen again from the garden centre today, and even though the manager has searched him every time he has taken sand to customers' cars, he has not found what Tom has stolen. Tom arrives home, opens his boot and out comes the stolen item that he has taken from work today. It is now stored in his garage with the rest of the stash taken over the last few weeks and months.

His garage now contains ten brand new wheelbarrows.

Every time Tom takes sand to customers' cars he is allowed to use a showroom wheelbarrow. The company hopes that the customer will be tempted to buy the barrow. If they don't, then Tom puts the new barrow in his car when no one is looking. By then he is past the product scanners and there is no CCTV in the car park.

Life is good for Tom.

Short Story 12: The Greek Artefact

Harry is a bright lad. He is now eighteen years old and has just passed his A levels and hopes to go to University to study Physics. Before that though he wants to travel around Greece and enjoy himself. He hopes to see the world by doing a little travelling. This is mainly to "find himself", as many people call it. He also wants to travel to get away from home, as he embarrassed his family and friends recently by having had a warning from the police for a minor theft from a local shop.

Having managed to earn a little money to travel Harry finds that he still has to generate some more. He decides that he can do this by organising children's parties. However he won't do this the usual way as he has a very innovative way to earn money. Some months ago he organised a children's party for a friend of the family. The gossip went around the school that it was a fantastic party for the kids. He became very popular with most of the school kids mums and dads because all the children were talking about him. Instead of doing magic tricks or making shaped balloons for a party he used the science he was taught at school to create experiments in the "party kitchen", to wow children. He gathered ideas from YouTube clips of science experiments and created a few more ideas himself. He brought these ideas to life and created a kids party full of sensory based experiments.

His favourite idea for a party experiment was to add add vinegar to a sodium bicarbonate solution which contains washing up liquid, creating a bubbling volcano. In another experiment, he did what he later called the glycerine trick. Glycerine is a harmless colourless liquid usually used with lemon juice as a sore throat remedy. In the experiment that he created, a glass of glycerine is used to hide a small colourless glass marble, which seems to disappear when submerged in the glycerine. This is because glycerine has the same properties of glass, so light goes through both and the glass marble seems to disappear in the glycerine. It looks like magic for kids. His third kitchen science trick which wowed the kids involved taking food colorant dyes (red, blue, green etc) and creating a rainbow effect in water where one colour sits on the other like a rainbow. This is easy to construct as every kitchen has a range a food dyes which all mums use when they make fancy birthday party cakes.

In total Harry had six kitchen experiments which he used at kids parties over the following months and the kids loved them, mainly because they were very visual and it looked like he was doing some magic, and also because the kids had never seen anything like it before. He made more money from tips from the parents than the actual fee he charged, so he soon had enough money for the Greek trip.

The day soon arrived for Harry to fly off to Greece. He had booked himself into a hotel near the airport in Greece for the first night so that he could have a good start to the trip. He would then search for a place to stay and find some simple bar work to tide him over.

The flight to Greece went well and the hotel that he stayed in for the first night was comfortable, so it seemed that he was all set for a good time in Greece.

Harry woke up on his first morning in Greece and took a look around Athens.

He then went to a small hotel in a local village near the capital, on the recommendation of his friend at home in England who had worked there for a few months. He would ask if they needed any bar work.

At the hotel Harry saw Stavros, the manager, who told him he had enough bar staff already, so a despondent Harry sat at the bar and had a drink himself, thinking on what to do next.

While having a drink at the bar he heard Stavros on the phone talking to an employee who couldn't make it in to work. He overheard that it was Maria, the bar girl who was phoning in sick. While Stavros was out at the back on the phone some people came up to the bar to order a drink, but there was no bar staff. It seemed to Harry that Maria must be the only bar staff and he had just overheard that she will not be in today so, Harry had a bright idea. He got up, went behind the bar and without the manager knowing he served the three people himself.

One of them asked for a cocktail which he never heard of, so he simply asked, in his cheeky way, what was in the cocktail and he would "magic it up as only the English can do". The customer laughed and told him how to make it. Harry then produced the cocktail with gusto. His manner made all the customers laugh and by the time Stavros the manager came back to the bar Harry told him that he had now served six customers and to look in the till for the money he had taken for him. Stavros was impressed and told Harry that if he can work all day today and do a good job then he can have Maria's job, as she was "pulling a sickie".

After a successful session behind the bar Harry was asked to come in the next day, which was a special day for the company as the small hotel were hosting the Athens Rainbow Crystal, a priceless artefact simply made from pure, clear glass, that shone like a rainbow when bright light was directed on it. People from all over Athens would come to the bar during the day to view it and the hotel manager had put it on a pedestal on the bar so that all could see. However he was concerned about its safety so he would keep an eye on it to make sure no-one would steal it.

As the day was an important and special one for the hotel Harry had been offered a room at the hotel for the night as it was to be a long and hopefully successful day for the hotel and Harry knew he would be behind the bar all day.

The big day arrived and the Stavros was excited. He would make much money from the bar as everyone who came to see the priceless artefact would buy a drink or two and probably order some food as well. He had mixed emotions though, as he knew there would be one or two criminals looking to steal the artefact if it wasn't looked after well. Stavros would keep his beady eye on it while the crystal was perched on the bar.

Harry had prepared for the all-day bar work session. He had a sandwich ready by the till and his drink was set, on the bar itself. It looked like a large neat vodka. He was allowed one free drink to keep him going. The morning went well. Many people were flooding in, not only buying drinks but buying food as well. Stavros would make good money today.

At eleven o'clock Stavros saw two known local crooks walk into the bar. This was obviously a worry but Stavros didn't want to turn people away or he might lose out on takings from the bar. One of the crooks was Giuseppe, a head shaven all-round bad guy, whose eyes were immediately fixed on the artefact. The other was Grecko, an unshaven has-been lowlife, who now roamed the streets looting whatever he could find. They both came into the bar at the same time and both were eyeing up the artefact.

Stavros knew that he would have to be alert to keep the artefact safe. It was for the moment still safely perched on the pedestal on the bar, with only those drinking at the bar and the bar staff near it. The two crooks were at the back of the bar well away from it, so for the moment he was happy.

Then suddenly, both crooks came forward to the bar at the same time. Was it a coincidence that they both needed a drink at the same time, or a pre-agreed pincer movement to get the artefact? Stavros wasn't sure.

Both crooks got to the bar at the same time. The two resident old gents at the bar cowered as they saw the crooks standing by their shoulder ordering a drink each. The crooks appeared frightening to the old gents. Harry moved his own drink away from the bar and served one of the crooks who ordered a beer. As he got the mans beer there was a commotion as the other crook dropped an empty bottle on the floor. Was it an accident? It hit the stone floor with a huge sounding crash which made everyone jump. A lady shouted to all to watch out for the bouncing shards of glass from the broken bottle. In the noise and confusion there was some rustling around the bar. Stavros looked up and saw the artefact was now missing from its pedestal. He shouted to everyone to stay where there were, but by then Giuseppe, the head shaven crook, was gone.

Stavros was devastated, he called the police. All the customers tried to help by figuring out what happened in the bottle smashing commotion. Even Grecko, the other crook, was taking part in the conversations to help.

While waiting for the police to arrive Stavros searched all the customers, to no avail. He was surprised that even Grecko hadn't got it. Grecko said that Guiseppe probably stole it and offered to go and find Giuseppe and get him to bring the artefact back, but Stavros didn't believe him and Grecko soon sneaked away. Stavros suspected they were both working together on this.

By the time the police came fifteen minutes later Stavros knew that Giuseppe and Grecko would be miles away and may have even sold the artefact by now.

An hour later, all the customers had gone. It was just Stavros who was present in the bar and Harry behind the bar tidying up. Otherwise, the bar was empty.

Stavros sat at one of the bar tables and harry got him a drink so that he could drown his sorrows. He might have made much money from food and drink sales today but Stavros had lost the priceless artefact.

Two hours later Harry, after a hard day's work behind the bar was resting in his hotel bedroom that he had been given for another night. He lay on the bed, his free drink sitting on the bedside table. It had been untouched all day. What looked like neat vodka, a colourless alcoholic beverage, was in fact colourless glycerine. Inside the glass, submerged under the liquid was the priceless Athens Rainbow Crystal artefact. The artefact was of course simply made from pure, clear glass, which has the same properties of glycerine and so was therefore neatly hidden from view inside the glass. He had popped it into his glass during the commotion at the bar.

His children's party trick had just won him a priceless artefact.

Harry smiled. Job done.

Short Story 13: The Train Journey

Julie loves train journeys. She is now on the train from London to Portsmouth & Southsea, and will get off at the fourth stop, in south London, to take her puppy Rex to their dog training class. Rex was also enjoying the train journey, quietly lying under her seat. He would soon nod off, she thought.

Julie had recently been made redundant from her job as a waitress in a café near home. Redundancy at the age of twenty-two was depressing for Julie, but at least she had put in some job applications recently so was hopeful of an interview or two soon. In the meantime, she was training Rex as best as she could by attending the set of six group classes she had enrolled on. The dog training classes had been going well and Rex had responded to Julies learned commands impressively. Border Collies are usually responsive so she hoped the training sessions would be really useful. She had to catch the Portsmouth and Southsea train to get to the dog training as she didn't drive, but that suited her as she loves trains. However, Julie couldn't possibly have predicted how this unusual train journey would end.

Julie liked people-watching and working out what people were like from their appearance. Sitting next to her on the train was a quiet middle-aged lady. She was very tanned so obviously spent time at the beach. She wore black trousers with a blue top. Julie couldn't make out the logo on the ladies blue top but noticed that it said "sea" at the end of it, with her scarf covering the rest. Julie guessed she came from Southsea as the train was going to Portsmouth and the lady probably worked in the tourist industry with a top like that. She thought it would be great to take Rex to the beach, maybe we should do that when he is fully trained, she thought. The lady introduced herself to Julie as Priscila, which she thought was a fancy name, so she was probably in a Marketing type role at work. She said she was going to Portsmouth for her day off.

Julie continued the people watching. Sitting opposite her was a kindly old man with a tweed jacket, shirt, old fashioned tie and smart trousers. It seemed to her that he was therefore a well-educated man. The old man had a posh accent and after a pleasant exchange of words he said

"I am very impressed with how well behaved your dog is."

Julie liked this old man. He was very engaging to talk to. She responded.

"Border Collies are easy to train and Rex has responded well to how the instructor has suggested that I work with him. Rex seems to understand actions better than words".

"How do you mean?" said the old man.

"Well" replied Julie "If I raise my arm as high as I can then Rex has learned to lie down, and if I hold my hand up in a halt sign then he will sit".

"That's impressive, but you better not do it now or else Rex will get up". The old man laughed. Julie smiled and continued.

"They teach you many commands to help you keep your dog under control and also a few first aid examples in case he gets ill. I didn't realise we would get first aid advice, so I asked a lot of questions at the end to learn a bit more. I don't want to be in a crisis with Rex and not know what to do."

"That's very sensible" said the old man.

Both the old man and the lady with the blue top smiled. They liked the idea that Julie was besotted with Rex and was trying to bond well with him. He was a very cute and engaging dog. The old man was smiling while the lady was on her phone, probably googling something about her visit to Portsmouth, Julie thought.

The old man continued. "What type of work do you do?"

Julie replied "I have just been made redundant from Bob's Café".

The old man's eyes lit up.

"That's a coincidence. I manage the coffee house at the other end of the street."

Julie got excited, maybe there's a job going, she wondered. Perhaps she can engineer a conversation with him about a job. Julie looked at the old man hopefully, but he changed the subject back to Rex.

"What other kind of first aid things did you learn at the training?"

"Oh, I learned what to do if Rex bleeds from a cut and how to apply a bandage. It's a bit more difficult to put a bandage on a dog than a human". The old man laughed again.

"Then in last week's session we did CPR in case of a heart attack"

"Wow" said the old man "I wouldn't have a clue what to do. Well done, that is impressive".

Julie was about to try to get the conversation back to the café, hoping that the old man might help her with a job, but then the old man got up as the train was stopping at a station.

"Well, this is my stop" he said. "Well done with the dog training and good luck with finding a job" and with that the old man suddenly got off the train.

Julie was dismayed, she had missed an opportunity to bluntly ask for a job.

The train moved off. It was only a minute now to her own stop. She looked at the middle-aged lady with the blue top, who smiled back at Julie.

Julie patted Rex on the head and said to him

"Come on Rex lets get to the training site".

She got up and so did Rex as the train slowed down towards her stop.

Then the tanned faced lady in blue said something strange.

"Have you got Airdrop on your iPhone?"

Julie was taken aback. Why would this lady want to send her a seaside photo from her phone to Julie's phone?

She said "Err, Yes I have"

The lady got her iPhone out and pressed a button.

"Why don't you accept this then?"

July looked at her own iPhone, which showed a caption that the lady had sent to her, so she accepted it. Then the doors of the train opened.

"Don't miss your stop" said the lady

Julie now frantically runs to the door with Rex and they both jump off the train onto the platform.

Now, Julie looks to see what the lady has sent her. It is a screenshot of an advert of some sort. How kind of the lady, Julie thinks. She must have googled for jobs while Julie was talking to the old man. Julie looks closer and see's that it is an advert for a "Dog/Cat Carer."

Wow, the lady must have been listening to her dog training conversation with the old man.

The train starts to move to go to the next stop and the lady in the carriage goes past Julie's eye line. As she passes by, the lady waves to Julie with a smile and as she does her blue top reveals the full logo of her blue shirt. Then it all makes sense to Julie. The logo says "Battersea Dogs home" which is where the advert location was.

Julie then realises that the "sea" that she had seen on her blue top wasn't from the word "Southsea" but from the word "Battersea."

So this lady must work at Battersea Dogs home in Windsor, thinks Julie.

Then, Julie see's something at the bottom of the advert which makes her jump. The hiring manager was someone called Priscila Stevens.

So, not only does the lady work there, she is the manager …..and she wants Julie to apply for the job!

Julie smiles. In trying to impress the old man for a job at a café she inadvertently impressed Priscila with a better job as a dog carer.

Perfect.
Julie looks down.
"Thank you Rex" she says.

Short Story 14: Did you hear about the burglary?

In the late 1980's minor crimes and especially disability fraud became a real problem. The government was losing a tremendous amount of money from people either committing petty crimes like shop burglary or claiming for a disability that they didn't have. Simple burglaries couldn't be dealt with quickly by the police as they had bigger fish to fry and fraudulent disability claims were lower down the priority list for some local authorities. What the public didn't know at the time was that the government had worked with the police to identify those who were thought to be either stealing from shops/local residents or claiming benefits when they did not a have a disability. These low-level criminals were being targeted now over an extensive period.

Dave was one such person who fitted the profile of this type of offender. He had a history of minor burglaries from shops or the homes of local residents. He was also claiming a disability benefit for being deaf when people who knew him knew his hearing was perfectly okay. Dave lives in a block of flats with his wife and daughters who are six and eight years old. He wasn't stupid and knew the police either ignored his burglary activities or just gave him a ticking off. He would only steal minor items worth twenty pounds or so from a shop and always seemed to get away with it.

Danwell Police station had now been set up with a dedicated police officer for a few months to catch people like Dave. Constable Jones was Danwells officer in charge and he had seen many CCTV clips of people committing minor crimes while wearing a hoody to conceal themselves, or some other coverage. He would then watch them walk back to their unkempt residential block of flats where many of these perpetrators seemed to live. Jones's role was to catch some of these criminals red handed while they either stole from a shop or claim benefits while pretending to be disabled, when they clearly were not from the CCTV footage.

Jones had already caught six people this week. He would view the CCTV footage beforehand then bring the culprit in to be interviewed at the police station and challenge them either with their burglaries or fraudulent claims. He would show them the evidence of the steal or prove that they didn't have a disability, then he would charge them. It was then the courts job to finish it off. It was easy for Jones to accomplish, and he got many positive results. He knows that some people are stupid. One lad last week even claimed a disability benefit for a missing right leg. As Jones ushered the lad into the station he showed the lad that he did indeed have both legs and then charged him for being a fraud!

It was Dave's turn now thought Jones. Jones knows Dave's record and earlier in the month he had questioned him at his house about a series of burglaries while his wife and two cute daughters kept quiet on the sofa. His daughters were very engaging but mum kept them silent. Dave did well at the time to also give the impression that he was deaf and he was a good lipreader. At the end of the discussion when Constable Jones told Dave he would soon lock him up, Sylvie, the younger daughter, ran up to dad and screamed "don't leave us dad" in fear, but Constable Jones told her that it wouldn't be today that dad would be locked up. It would be another day. Jones got up and left thinking it was cute that Sylvie was scared for her dad at the thought of being locked up. It's a shame that nice kids belonged to such horrible parents, he thought.

It is now a week later and Jones is back at the station and thinking about how to nail Dave. He already had CCTV evidence of a number of Dave's minor crimes inside shops. Dave was known to steal from shops or local residents, not just occasionally but a few times a week, so it would be easy to call him into the station and show him the CCTV evidence. Dave did all this while claiming to be deaf and receiving a large disability payment. He clearly wasn't deaf as Jones could tell from CCTV footage outside the betting shop that Dave could hear the traffic as he crossed the road.

Jones wants to nail Dave but the burglaries will only give him a fine. However, if he can prove his deaf fraudulent claim then he can get him banged up for a much punchier sentence. Jones now watches the CCTV carefully. Although he has enough previous burglary related evidence to call Dave in right now he will just see what he is up to today. It is close to Christmas so perhaps he will steal something for his two daughters. Dave is in the street and has just walked up and past the local fruit and vegetable shop. Sure enough, just outside the shop he takes some of the fruit on offer outside the store, fills his pockets, and walks on. Another piece of evidence for Jones.

Before he calls Dave into the police station he has to prepare. He wants everything to count, and he wants a tough sentence, not just a fine. His new role means he has the facility to setup the station as he likes so that he can complete Dave's demise, which he does with the help of another officer.

Dave is called in. He is smart but doesn't realise that he has just been caught on CCTV outside the fruit shop and is even eating an apple which he stole, so he is in some trouble now.

In the interview room Jones sits opposite and facing Dave behind a table, with the door slightly open. Dave has his back to the open door and he is facing Constable Jones. The radio can be clearly heard through the door behind Dave. The police in the office are listening to Christmas songs on Radio One.

Jones charges him with claiming benefits for being deaf and also six counts of theft from various places. The radio continues to play Christmas songs while Jones talks him through the thefts, one by one.

Dave denies everything of course. He is careful to look straight ahead and lip read to make it look like he can understand while being deaf. He has practiced this many times.

Unfortunately for Dave, he, like the public, never realised there were so many CCTV cameras that were around in the 1980's so when Constable Jones talks Dave through the six counts of theft, including the latest apple that he is currently eating, Dave is a little surprised at the amount of evidence that the police have on him and is now slightly worried. Will all these pieces of evidence add up to a big penalty? However, on reflection Dave is sure, from pub talk, that these minor thefts can only result in a fine, which he won't pay of course. He is positive that he won't get a tough sentence from his fraudulent claim of being deaf. Constable Jones knows that that will only happen if he can prove Dave is a fraud by not being deaf.

Dave is still putting on a good show of pretending to be deaf and not being able to hear the Radio One Christmas songs coming through the door behind him. He smiles inwardly as he thinks Constable Jones is trying to trick him into singing along with the songs, which would mean he can hear them. Oh no you won't catch me out, Dave thinks. Just focus on lip reading and all will be well.

As the Christmas songs continue to permeate the gap through the door behind Dave, Jones finishes talking him through the evidence they have for his thefts. Dave keeps still and quiet focusing on Jones's lips.

Jones has the advantage of seeing over Dave's shoulder, through the open door and waits for his moment for when all is ready.

It is now time, thinks Jones.

Constable Jones tells Dave that he has all the evidence he needs and with a loud, stern and forceful voice he tells Dave it is now time for him to be locked up in jail.

In response to this, Dave suddenly hears behind him a scream from a little girl he recognises as Sylvie shouting

"No…daddy!" and in a reactive moment Dave turns around to see his younger daughter sitting by a policeman in the office looking and listening to them. Dave instantly realises he has been set up. He had turned around on hearing his daughter behind him, which confirmed that he is not deaf. He now notices the video camera in the roof of the interview room pointing at him. It has captured him turning around as his daughter screamed. His fraudulent deaf claim had been smashed.

Constable Jones smiles. Another one nicked.

Short Story 15: Eating Like a Gannet

In the 1920's there were many British explorers who would run to different parts of the world to find new places, animals or environments that hadn't been discovered.

Dr McTavish is one of these explorers. McTavish is a 20th century Biologist and is keen on all forms of the animal or plant kingdom, whether it be new or old.

In 1921 an extraordinary secret committee of Biologists was established. Their role was to research into all things living. One part of this work was to set up an expedition to establish whether the recent claim in the papers was true, which was whether the Dodo bird was really extinct or not. Sitings of this bird had been seen on a small Hawaiian island. The name of the island was kept secret for obvious reasons.

It is now six months after the trip, and Dr McTavish is sitting in the study armchair beside the roaring fire one evening, contemplating what had happened over the last few weeks following this visit to the island to spot the Dodo.

It had been eventful and positive trip. As the lead Biologist McTavish led a team of three students and visited this undisclosed Hawaiian island. McTavish is not an adventurous person; drinks a bit, is a little bit overweight and doesn't get out much. So a working trip in the Hawaiian sun certainly boosted morale somewhat especially as McTavish is also a keen bird watcher. While there with the students they collected plenty of biological specimens as well as checking out the existence of the Dodo.

In the armchair McTavish thought about the Dodo. It is

a bird that was thought to be extinct in the 1600's, but two pairs had been seen on this small, beautiful island.

It was important to check it out. However, the problem had been that the island was only inhabited by a tribe of cannibals. The cannibals ate nothing but human flesh or Gannet flesh, a seabird. In McTavish's party of six they stayed with the Cannibal tribe and of course ate Gannet meat while the cannibal hosts ate human flesh. They did take a revolver with them just in case, but it all worked out well.

McTavish and the team had never eaten Gannet meat before, and of course would never consider human flesh. That would be repulsive and would be left to the cannibals.

They found that gannet meat had a pleasant taste. McTavish's view was that humans eat birds such as chicken, turkey, quail here in Europe and they all have a lovely taste. Gannet is also a bird and has a similar taste to turkey so why not try it? It turned out to be a pleasant experience for the team.

McTavish smirked inwardly by the fireside while remembering one of the younger Biologists who said that he would join the cannibals one evening in eating human flesh. The young man went white faced and silent when the food came. He couldn't do it in the end.

While on the island Dr McTavish and the team formed a search party and went to search for the Dodo. They indeed found a pair, at a distance. They were delighted. The Dodo is an ungainly bird and although it was amazing to see the Dodo pair, they soon disappeared from sight. However, they saw them for just enough to take a photo and bring the proof home to England. Photos in the 1920's weren't great but it worked as excellent proof that the Dodo was not extinct and the party came back to England with huge publicity.

All this happened a few months ago. Now, sitting by the fire McTavish is recollecting the trip because todays Daily Telegraph paper, sitting on the table, has an article describing a café which has opened up in town. Their news is that they are selling gannet salads, using gannet meat obtained from the

Scottish coast. This has excited McTavish and the team loved the taste of Gannet so a trip to the café would be excellent.

The next day McTavish calls the expedition team members one by one to ask if they want to visit the cafe, but only Pat Robinson can come. Pat is very keen to eat Gannet again. They agree to meet in the café.

A week later they meet inside the café, greet each other and quickly order the Gannet salad as they are hungry.

They catch up on gossip while their Gannet salad arrives.

After one bite the Doctor and student both stop chewing and look at each other quizzically.

"This isn't gannet meat" said Dr McTavish

The student agrees.

The manager is nearby and McTavish queries the food telling him that it is not gannet meat.

"Oh yes, it is gannet" the manager replies.

"But this tastes nothing like I had on the Island," says McTavish, looking at Pat.

While McTavish and the student look at each other they both realise at the same time that the food on their plate today must be gannet meat, but that means on the island they must have been given something else to eat by the tribe. If it wasn't gannet meat they ate on the island then it must have been….

The student goes white as he realises that he had been eating human flesh on the island.

They both leave the café shocked.

The student returns home to his family in London.

Dr McTavish returns home as well, also in London.

McTavish then did what any reasonable person would do after being upset unnecessarily. She went back home to her husband for a cuddle.

Short Story 16.: A Smile Means Everything.

This is a true story which happened to the author. All names have been changed for this story.

It was a cold wet miserable evening at Amsterdam Schiphol airport in 1990. Helen worked for a UK company who had offices near Amsterdam so she occasionally had to fly there from Heathrow to meet up with her Dutch colleagues. Although the visits were good fun they were very long days so by the time she got to Schiphol airport to come home she was exhausted.

All she really wanted was a swift passage through the airport and have a nap on the plane on its way back to Heathrow. Tonight would be difficult evening though.

There are a few major airlines you can use to travel to and from Amsterdam. I won't say which airline Helen used on this day, the reason for which will become apparent. When travelling back to England from Amsterdam Helen usually catches the 6pm flight home, but on this day she had to work late and so had to catch the 8.30pm flight home; which was the last flight with this airline. Not a good idea. We all know that flights are rarely on time and tonight the weather is appalling, so it is unlikely that Helen will take off on time for her flight.

Helen arrives at the airport in Amsterdam and there is a queue at the check in desk. She gets a coffee and looks out of the huge airport windows and notices the worsening weather. It's been snowing most of the afternoon and now the airport is packed with people, which suggests that flights have and will be delayed. This doesn't look good, she need to find a plasma screen. The plasma screens are full of the single word "Delayed". Helen looks up to see that her flight is one of only a few that are not delayed. Not yet, but surely a delay is inevitable she thinks.

Helen has her coffee and sees two classic stereotyped people also having coffee nearby, talking to each other at the next table. One is clearly a Dutch lady. She wears a checked jacket, the type that the Dutch typically wear, and spoke fabulous English. She was talking to her business colleague, a typical English business lady who was simply embarrassing to any English person nearby. She was dressed a little pompously and spoke to the Dutch lady in such a condescending way. Even the waitress who brought over her coffee got both a look of distain from her and a rude, impatient comment as well. Helen is embarrassed to listen to a bolshie English business person demanding everything from everyone, so she gets up and goes shopping before moving onto the check-in gate.

After visiting the shops Helen joins the queue at the check-in gate and sees that the weather is awful and flights are changing to "Delayed" every minute. When joining the queue she didn't realise who was directly in front of her. It's that embarrassing English business lady. As they are both English Helen assumes she is probably on flight 666 as well. Knowing Helens luck the lady will catch the last seat on the plane and she will miss out.

At last the business lady gets to the front and speaks to the lovely airline lady at the check in desk, but Helen can't believe what she says....or perhaps she can.

"Right" the English business lady starts, "I am on flight 666 in economy class and I want an upgrade."

Helen can't believe her impolite manner. The check in lady is obviously used to this and looks straight at her and replies seamlessly.

"Sorry madam, flight 666 is delayed by fifty minutes. We are not checking in just yet. Can you return in half an hour please?"

Helens heart sinks. A delay. Fifty minutes will probably turn into a longer wait. The business lady complains…. surprise, surprise. Then she picks her bag up and storms off.

So, Helen thinks to herself what to do now. She is on flight 666 as well, so should she get another coffee and wait? Then, suddenly Helen realises that the business lady has gone and the check in desk lady is now looking at her.

"Can I help you?" she says.

Helen replies "Thanks, but I am also on flight 666 as well as that lady, I'll come back in half an hour, as you suggested."

"No" the check in lady replies "I can check you in now. Your flight is leaving on time" and before Helen could think, the check-in lady takes her ticket and passport off her to check her in.

It takes Helen a while to work out what is going on. What's with the sudden change of mind? The lady recognises her confusion and gives Helen a "knowing smile".

She says "It's okay, I can check you in……you were polite and said "thank you.""

Then she carries on with the paperwork.

Its not just a picture that describes a thousand words. A "knowing smile" does as well.

Her smile meant "be polite and I'll help you, but mess with me and….".

Helen caught the flight. The English lady wasn't seen at the gate and Helen didn't see her get on or off the plane, so she probably didn't make it back to England that night.

Morel of the story: Politeness costs nothing, but it rewards.

Helen loves the Dutch, especially their airline staff.

Short Story 17: Caught in the Act

Alex and Zac are brothers. Orphaned at a young age they were placed with a family who looked after them well. As the brothers were twins their new parents sometimes dressed them in similar clothes which comically confused friends of the family. However, those who knew them well could tell them apart by a slight difference in their stature, where one of them had a more upright stance than the other.

They now live together as young adults in their south London flat and tend to keep themselves to themselves. Of course, now that they are adults they wear different styles of clothes so they appear as clearly very different people.

Alex has more rounded shoulders and therefore tends to slouch when walking compared to Zac. Zac is aware of his upright posture and continually does upper body exercises to improve it further and keep both tall and physically fit. This means Zac now walks with a more upright stance. He knows this and wants to make use of this fact soon.

Alex doesn't look after himself well. He appears undernourished, has low self-esteem and is known to the police as a persistent minor thief. He doesn't smoke, on medical grounds, but he makes up for it in the pub by drinking far more than he should with his friends, while eating unhealthy food and watching football.

Zac is the smart one. He managed to get a few GCSE's at school and got a job at an accountancy firm where he is training to be a qualified accountant. He loves football, is a big City fan and from a young age has supported the blues, whereas Alex is a United fan and shouts for the reds. They are both passionate about football and when a game is on television in the pub they are engrossed in it. The reds verses the blues is the only brotherly disagreement they have really and sometimes their passion does get a bit out of hand. When the two teams play each other they make an evening of it by going to the pub and sitting with their respective mates in the pub. The reds fans sit by the bar and the blues fans by the door. The bragging rights goes to the supporters of the winning team.

Zac knows that he smokes far too much, but is trying to cut down and improve his overall health. Unlike Alex, he hasn't been in trouble with the police yet, but they know both lads well on paper, especially Alex, after his recent criminal antics.

Living together has been frustrating for Zac as he has started to try and lead an independent life. He is tired of Alex getting into trouble with the police. As the days go by Zac does his best to cut down on cigarettes and beers and improve his overall lifestyle. He also tries to improve his posture further by continuing the exercises to keep his back straighter. It is these exercises that have helped him walk with a better posture, while the stooped shouldered Alex cannot be bothered to improve his image. Alex simply wants to spend time in the pub watching the reds win at football.

Zac now thinks it's time to get rid of his brother. He knows that every few months Alex succumbs to some form of theft and Zac knows that he isn't very bright. Alex thinks that if he wears a hoody then even if the police see his face they wouldn't tell if it was him or Zac who committed the crime. He is not aware of the difference in their statures and he doesn't realise that the police can tell by the stoop of his shoulders which brother he is. Alex usually ends up with minor fines after his crimes, but one day he will go to jail if he is not careful.

Zac realises that he now knows how to get rid of his brother. Before he goes to the pub to see his blues side play football he will steal something and frame Alex. Now is the time to do it. He buys a cheap hoody identical to Alex's, then goes to the local shop and steals an expensive item. A few meters before he enters the shop he changes from his upright stance to a stooped stance to mimic Alex. This is of course for the CCTV camera in the shop. He has practised this for days so he is good at impersonating Alex's posture. Zac wears a cap and gloves, identical to those his brother wears. Then he deliberately shows his face to the CCTV camera just outside the shop. The police will instantly think it is Alex who has stolen the item.

Zac assumes that the police will arrest Alex, who has no alibi as Zac has given Alex a job to do in the flat. This makes sure Alex is alone in the flat when the dirty deed is done so no one can support his whereabouts.

The call comes into the police station that an expensive item has been stolen from the shop. The police immediately look at the footage of the CCTV camera near the shop.

The CCTV camera clearly shows someone in a hoody looking like Alex coming out of the shop in a shifty manner.

However, Inspector Jones isn't too sure if the man in the CCTV picture is Alex or Zac. He is concerned that the man in the hoody looked up at the camera as if he deliberately wanted to be seen. He knows the brothers well on paper, even though he hasn't actually met Zac yet, and he is aware that Alex isn't clever enough to play tricks with a CCTV camera. Zac is though, which makes Inspector Jones suspicious. He now wonders if Zac is trying to frame his brother.

To confirm his suspicions, the astute Inspector Jones decides to look at footage of other street CCTV cameras nearby. These show that the hooded man isn't stooping now but has a very straight back, something that the stooped Alex cannot do. Jones concludes that the hooded man must therefore be Zac and he is up to something.

Meanwhile, Zac having stolen the item from the shop, decides to dispose of it and then rushes to the pub to watch the football on the huge plasma TV screen. He again mimics Alex's posture and hopes that if anyone in the pub sees him they will think that he is Alex, with stooped shoulders. This will incriminate Alex as it will look like Alex has stolen something and then hidden in the pub.

Inspector Jones is still suspicious but needs to find a way to be sure that it is Zac who is the actual culprit. He needs to be absolutely positive before any arrest. Jones made a mess of an arrest last week and now wants to be definitely sure that if he arrests Zac and charges him for the theft, then he has got it right this time.

Jones has seen the footage of the CCTV cameras showing the hooded man went straight to the pub. That makes sense. The brothers love both football and unhealthy food, so the hoody man is probably having a drink and watching the football to hide from the police. If Jones can get to the pub quickly and prove that it is actually Zac in the pub then he has his man.

Jones, in plain clothes goes to pub immediately.

When he is there he realises that he has the advantage because he and Zac have not met Zac before, so Zac doesn't know that Inspector Jones is a policeman.

Jones sits at the other end of the pub to Zac, who is still pretending to be Alex by stooping his shoulders as he sups his beer and watches the football on TV.

Jones watches him intently. He has to think of a way to prove it is Zac.

Then he has an idea.

Jones sees that Zac is drinking the same real ale as he is, so he goes up to Zac and introduces himself as a fellow real ale drinker. Jones then shakes his hand. As he does this Zac gives something away which proves to Jones that he is not Alex. Jones smiles to himself, makes his excuses, and goes back to his seat. He is sure now.

Zac is now suspicious of Jones. People don't do that kind of thing in a pub like this. He gets ready to make his escape now that he has shown his face in the pub, and hopefully people think he is Alex.

Meanwhile, Jones sits down at the other end of the pub to Zac. He now knows that it is indeed Zac that he has met.

When he shook hands he saw that Zac's fingers have yellow nicotine stains so this man must be Zac because Alex doesn't smoke, on medical grounds, so he wouldn't have yellow fingers.

However, Jones needs a second piece of evidence to be sure that this man is Zac and also to add weight to the conviction. There is one other way he can be sure who it is that he is looking at, but he has to wait, and wait, and wait, for it to happen. He also realises that Zac is itching to leave the pub, so Jones hopes it will happen soon.

Then it does happen. Zac gives himself away.

There is a loud roar from the football on the television screen as Zac's blues have scored against the reds of United. Zac spontaneously shouts in joy, then realises his mistake and sits down quickly.

Alex supports the reds and wouldn't cheers for a blues goal, but Zac would.

Everyone in the pub now realises that it is Zac in the pub and not Alex. Everyone looks and stares at Zac.

Everything from the shop steal to the pub visit has been captured on CCTV so Jones walks up to Zac and tells him he is nicked.

Short Story 18: The Lifeguard

Jim is in a happy mood as he is on holiday at Croyde Bay in the southeast of England. It's the first time he has taken time off work for a few years so the idea of lying on a sandy beach in the sun for a few days is very appealing. He might even take in some surfing lessons as he would love to learn how to do it. The forecast is for good weather so his relaxation time should be fun, but in this moment of happiness he doesn't realise what is about to happen to him over the next week.

The start of the holiday turns out to be perfect. The chalet that Jim has rented is neat and suits his purposes well. The nearby beach at Croyde is beautiful with huge stretches of sand. Even the weather has proved to be correct with plenty of sunshine and of course he can enjoy those long daylight hours in June for some evening entertainment.

The next day brings further sunshine and Jim arrives at the beach. There are not many people there just yet as he is so early but he finds a good position to lay down both his towel and his small surfboard on the sand. He sprawls on the sand and enjoys the warmth of the rays from the sun. Jim nods off for a while as he relaxes.

When Jim wakes up many people have arrived on the beach and although he has plenty of room he can see that it will get even busier later today. The beach is well set up. There is a lifeguard station in the middle of the sandy beach so that if someone gets caught up in the swell of the sea while swimming, they can be on hand to perform an immediate rescue. There are also plenty of shops nearby to keep people well fed and watered.

Two lifeguards are on duty today. Jim smiles to himself as the two lads are very different to look at. One is tall, slender and good looking, wearing those one-way-view sunglasses that make lads seem cool, just like in the Baywatch films. Jim thinks that the lad fancies himself a bit too much. The other lifeguard, who is being trained to be a full lifeguard, is a short, tubbier lad and in Jim's opinion isn't really one for the girls. Not that anyone cares when they need rescuing of course, as long as the Lifeguards are good at their job. Both lifeguards have long, rectangular shaped surfboards. The good-looking lad has a blue one and the shorter lad has a red one. He wanders if the colours represent seniority.

Jim sits up and feels the need for a drink and a short wander; he looks around now and observes many people enjoying the sun and sand. The man next to him has a large, hairy belly and is asleep on his ugly red blow up Lilo.

Jim wants to get a coffee so he makes his way past the man to get to the promenade shop. As Jim walks past the man he accidentally knocks over the man's chocolate flake ice-cream and it is now coated with sand. Jim apologises but the man waves him off angrily and tells him to go away. Jim gets to the shop, buys a large coffee and returns to his towel to drink it.

Once Jim has consumed the steaming coffee he looks at his watch and as it is now midday and he is hot then it is perhaps time to have a go on his new surf board. He won't actually surf as he doesn't know how to do it well, but he will lie on his front and use his arms to paddle in and out with the waves. He enters the water which is still cold from the winter chill. He paddles out to sea using his arms and passes the flag that warns the public of the powerful currents. He doesn't realise it but he is now in possible danger.

Jim enjoys paddling in the waves but after twenty minutes or so he doesn't realise how much energy he has used up and becomes exhausted. He also doesn't realise that while paddling into the waves the strong current has taken him dangerously into the deep sea, well away from the beach and he hasn't the strength now to paddle back. All the people on the beach are far away and they appear to look as small as ants now. He becomes panicky as he tries to paddle back but the current is taking him even further out. He becomes even more tired and frantic and then suddenly in his haste to paddle harder he falls off the surfboard into the sea and takes a large gulp of water. Jim is now cold, weak, hungry and scared. He hangs onto the surfboard while spluttering to breathe, but he cannot swim well and is soon struggling to stay above the water. He has taken in much salty water. He grabs his surfboard and holds on for dear life.

More minutes pass and he now hasn't the strength to use his arms other than to hold onto the surfboard. He can only hope that the lifeguard will have seen him flapping and will come and save him. He has accidentally drunk lots of salt water which makes him even more thirsty and disorientated. In his delirious state he tries to stay calm. Jim just hopes that the Lifeguard will come soon.

Jim now summons the energy to get back on the surfboard and into a lying position but in doing so he is even more tired and now has double vision through exhaustion and dehydration. His sight might be impaired, but he can just about see the blur of a rectangle approaching him. He is relieved now as he hopes one of the Lifeguards will get to him soon and rescue him. With his tired head resting on the surfboard he is now annoyed at himself for thinking negative thoughts about the cool dude lifeguard and now hopes he will save his life.

Jim's senses are getting even more dizzy now and his double vision is giving him a headache, but he can now feel that he is being rescued and can sense a hand grapple with his arm and get him in a position to be rescued.

Twenty minutes later Jim is lying on the sandy beach shore with two ambulance men attending him. He has had water pumped out of his stomach and Jim soon recovers consciousness; he is then taken to the hospital, which is only a mile away. Jim recovers in hospital and is discharged that evening.

The next day he wants to thank the lifeguard. He is

embarrassed to have got into trouble and he feels that he should give his thanks to the young man. He gets to the beach and see's the same two lads on Lifeguard duty.

Jim walks up to the dude lifeguard and thanks him for saving his life yesterday afternoon. The Lifeguard takes off his sunglasses, tells Jim that he didn't rescue him as he went off duty at midday so wasn't around to rescue him in the afternoon.

Jim is shocked and then realises that it must have been the shorter lifeguard who saved him, after all he was the one who had the red surfboard. He looks to his right and sees the shorter lifeguard and so walks up to him. Jim feels bad about thinking negative thoughts about this young lads stature, because this young man has now saved his life. When Jim reaches the young man he thanks him for his help. However, the young lad tells Jim that he has never seen him before, and the only rescue he did yesterday was for a little four-year-old boy.

Jim is bemused now. While walking away from the lifeguard station he thinks back to what he saw and heard when he was on his surfboard yesterday. He vaguely remembers now that whoever rescued him had a rectangular shaped red surfboard so surely it was the shorter lifeguard lad who rescued him?

The shorter lifeguard shouts and calls Jim back to him. When Jim reaches him the lad points in the direction of the shore to a man and tells him that he saw that person go to help someone yesterday so it may have been he who helped Jim.

Jim looks over to where the lifeguard is pointing to and sees lying on his red rectangular Lilo the man with the large, hairy belly. Jim goes over to him and thanks him for saving his life.

The large man tells Jim that the lone lifeguard was busy rescuing a young boy so he stepped in to help. Jim is surprised but thanks him again. It must have been his red Lilo that he saw when he was in trouble, thinking it was a red surfboard.

Jim thanks him again and asks if he can do anything to

say thank you. The man gruffly accepts Jim's thanks and then raises his hand to show the wooden stick of a completed ice lolly. He suggests another one of these would do the trick, this time without the sand.

Short Story 19: Office Life

So, we now come to the last two stories. These were the two that Uncle Chris had chosen to read to the two grandchildren. It was another cold winter's night high up in the snowy Welsh mountains. Uncle Chris, sitting in front of his roaring log fire, was enjoying warmth of the fire of his luxury log cabin, which was situated halfway up one of the highest mountains in Wales.

Uncle Chris was enjoying a whisky in front of the fire and reminiscing to the grandchildren about past stories that he always enjoyed sharing. He loved to tell stories to them, all of which had a little twist that would have them fooled. He was ready to begin.

"Sandy and Ash, you might go into industry when you grow up. If that's the case you will be interested in this story about office life. You go through many emotions when you have to deal with different types of people in a working office. It's about a group of six girls who started working life after college. They were friends, but things got a little strained over time as odd events happened. It wasn't so much who was doing it, but how to catch her at it."

Uncle Chris continued. "Sam, Helen, Ruth, Carrie, Tammy and Babs were all working for an insurance company in the centre of London, right next to London Bridge. Ruth, Carrie and Tammy all started at the same time. They all came from the Manchester area so had a strong Manchurian accent. Ruth, the red head, was typically short of patience and wanted to progress with her career so that she could earn some serious money. Tammy wasn't really bothered about career life but was more interested in life outside work, especially if lads were involved. Carry was the quiet one who would make sure that everyone in the office was happy. They were the best of friends. Helen and Babs joined the company a few weeks after. Helen, another career minded girl, was studious, calculating and quiet, but determined. She was nicknamed "stone face" by the others.

Babs was a sharp introduction to the group. She called a spade a spade. No messing. She was also by far the best sports person, keeping herself fit. There wasn't a sport centre within fifty miles that she hadn't visited.

Then, the final and recent addition to the group was Sam. She was quirky and a bit naive, but knew how to get what she wanted in life. A strange mix of office girls indeed!"

The grandchildren were captivated. They both knew a Sam at school.

Uncle Chris continued. "Their office was a relatively small one, just about big enough for the six of them. They each had their own desk space, a kind of office setup where three of them faced the other three with a divider in between. So it was quite intimate for a working environment. At the other end of the office was a small kitchenette and a seating area to relax.

Life was reasonably good for a while. However, Sam the new starter, who had only been there two months, didn't really fit in. Since she had started, a series of strange things started to happen, where people's possessions started to go missing."

"Head office had recently told them that they were having a new starter. Eli was a disabled teenager, wheelchair bound after a car accident. She was intelligent, sharp and above all excellent on the computer. Her legs might not work but she was five times quicker at typing on the computer than the six office girls. The girls had previously complained to the manager at the Leeds head office that they had too much paperwork to do (which involved writing reports on the computer and none of the girls were very good at typing quickly on the computer). So head office got Eli in, who would ask the girls to individually dictate the reports to her and then Eli would speedily write them up on the computer. She would support them all, but report into Sam, which added another bit of tension between the girls."

"Eli arrived on her first day and settled in well. She was asked to bring her own recorder so that the girls could dictate their morning reports before she arrived at midday. Then Eli would in her own time listen to the recordings and type them all up quickly. When Eli arrived on her first day she showed Sam her old dilapidated dictaphone that she had. Sam thought it was a bit old fashioned but if it worked and she didn't need to type reports then she was happy. Sam tried it out, pressed the record button, the little red light came on and she spoke. The unit recorded the words of the report and Eli then typed it up. Sam was impressed, the process works, and it will save the six girls much time. Over the next few weeks reports were completed by Eli very quickly and she became a useful and liked member of the team."

"Eli did soon get to hear about the strange goings on with the missing possessions and was a little concerned that it might be Sam who was starting to steal things in the office, as Sam appeared a bit odd to her."

Uncle Chris enjoyed being with the grandchildren and saw they were getting absorbed in the story so he continued. "It all came to a head on a cold March Monday morning when a series of strange things happened over a two hour period just before Eli arrived for work.

The day started well, all the girls had coffee together and shared a joke or two. Sam then got ready to dictate a report for when Eli arrived later in the day. Sam set the dictaphone to record and the little red light came on. She then started to talk into the machine, began with the title and introduction but after a few seconds Ruth screamed out loud from her office chair and pointed to the other side of the office. The girls thought that Ruth, the red headed stroppy girl, was being a drama queen again, but on looking saw that the toaster was on fire in the kitchenette. Babs had put some bread in it and it must have got stuck. All six girls raced over to the toaster and flapped, except Carrie who calmly got a wet tea towel and put it over the flames, having already turned the toaster switch off at the mains. She then turned off the smoke alarms as they soon would be activated. All calmly done and typically Carrie. Problem sorted."

"However, when the girls returned to their desks Ruth exclaimed that her purse had been stolen from her desk. Someone had stealthily taken it when all were rushing to the toaster. Sam was the last one to get to the toaster incident so Babs thought it was she who was the thief. Babs doesn't mix her words and well, she is always suspicious, so for the first time accusations were made out loud. Babs accused Sam of stealing the purse and also committing misdemeanours that had happened in the past, which no one had previously spoken about. She said she would be talking to Head Office about what had happened. Sam denied the accusations and there was a nasty atmosphere in the air now as they all looked at each other in the kitchenette. Sam had got the blame and she was feeling persecuted.

Calm Carrie suggested they chill out and have a coffee break saying that perhaps it wasn't stolen but mislaid, after all Carrie suspected someone other than Sam. That suggestion kept the peace for a while."

"Any idea who the thief was?" said Uncle Chris?

"I thought it was Sam, but she seems too sensible." said the grandchildren simultaneously.

"Yes, well you are right, it wasn't Sam. Helen was the culprit and Sam had indeed suspected her. On that Monday morning Helen used the toaster distraction to pinch the purse, knowing that everyone suspected Sam as no one really liked her. Sam suspected it was Helen but the problem was that she thought no one else agreed with her.

She didn't realise that in fact some of the other girls suspected that it was Helen as well, but no-one could actually catch Helen out. Sam was desperately trying to think of how to trap Helen and then she would get the respect of the others."

Uncle Chris continued. "So, Sam went back to her desk as she wanted to continue the dictation after the toaster incident. She wanted to finish quickly as Eli would arrive soon. Sam got to her desk, sat down and started working.

Helen had also walked back to her desk, which was opposite Sam's. Helen was convinced she had got away with the steal, with the purse hidden away out of sight and the blame with Sam. Helen sat down, opposite Sam and glanced over to see that the other four girls were at the other end of the office by the kettle, too far away to hear. Sam, who had started working a few minutes ago had an idea. She thought it was Helen who stole the purse so she quietly asked her if she had in fact committed the crime. Helen leant over towards Sam and whispered "Yes I did steal it but you won't persuade the others that it wasn't you, they all hate you!" With that, Helen smiled and sat down".

"Sam leaned back in her own chair also with a smile on her face as she glanced towards her desk at the small little red flashing recording light of the Dictaphone, as she hadn't finished dictating yet. The girls can listen to that later, she thought, and so can head office."

Uncle Chris leant back and enjoyed another whisky while the grandchildren smiled.

Short Story 20: Nurses know best

Of course, the two grandchildren asked Uncle Chris for another story.

It was now late in the evening and although it was, dark, wet and windy outside in the Welsh mountains it was warm and cosy in front of the chalet fire. The grandchildren were ready for another twisty story from Uncle Chris, who was sitting facing them.

Uncle Chris started. "Sharon, Sue, Hilary and Judy were junior nurses at St. Stephens hospital. They have known each other since primary school. All four went through school, college and then graduated together as fully-fledged junior nurses. They soon all got into St Stephens hospital and started working together under one roof. Perfect for all four of them. They were a team and they would stick together.

After working hard for a couple of months the four nurses arranged to have a day off together, which they needed to recharge their batteries now that COVD was quietening down. As the day approached, little did they know what excitement was to happen when their chill-out day arrived."

He continued. "It was Sharon who initially suggested the day out in London to all, while munching on some fruit pastilles, her only unhealthy habit. She was good at suggesting ideas. Hilary smiled that lovely smile and agreed that they should do something special. Sue voted for the wine bar to start off the day and Judy thought that a quick session in the spa would raise spirits, followed by coffee and cake in a cafe. They agreed that a stroll in London would then be followed by some evening Spanish tapas, and who knows, there they might find some admirers (as all of them were single). Hilary had an admirer last week and previous to that,

Judy fluttered her eyes at a few lads in the pub, but nothing serious materialised. Bland nurses uniforms don't do much for getting a partner."

"So, when their day off arrived they got themselves ready early in the morning. Sue dressed in a stunning "if looks could kill" outfit. She tires easily; standing up all day in size 5 shoes while being a little heavy of foot makes it tough for her. The odd cigarette and Pinot Noir don't help energy levels either. Hilary put on those new white flashy trousers, the one's bought yesterday. The pastel-coloured shoes were a clash but that's just Hilary. Sharon wore something simple, she keeps herself to herself usually and is quite understated in her attire but very observant. Judy is the loud one of the four and she wore a typically shouty green outfit."

"The first stop was the mid-morning wine bar of course. They all like Pinot so there was no debate there. Here the group conversation started, no one was going to ruin their day. With glass in hand Judy suggested that Hilary should do Pilates sometime in her spare time. Hilary had cracked a pelvis as a youngster when falling off a horse, so jumped at the Pilates idea, as a local group was starting soon.

Sharon suggested to Sue that she starts yoga as she continually loses energy with work and needs a way to recoup that. Conversation then led to using the spa, which was great for all of them. It was simply a dip in the pool really but Judy and Sue in particular really appreciated it."

"That was followed in the next street by a walk and then coffee and cake, which was a must, of course. More calories, but they will burn them off at work in hospital the next day. Then, a walk through the London parks led to a tapas bar. They were keen for this meal mainly because everyone was "on show" and who knows what romantic surprises might come from a Spanish eatery."

"The tapas was good, especially the evening cocktails. Sue was now feeling and looking five years younger compared to earlier in the day. Judy was loving it also. The tapas food was great and yes there were a few admiring looks, especially for Hilary and Sharon (having nice legs always helps)."

"After another long walk through Hyde park the finale was to be a late coffee at Costa, but before that the four nurses would need to be "on the ball" as things were happening in the town centre now. The dropping of COVID restrictions meant that in the centre of London people were boozing heavily in the pubs and it was now late evening, so time for them to come out onto the streets after a heavy night of drinking."

Uncle Chris continued. "The four nurses needed to walk through Soho to get to Costa. They would walk through the melee of teenagers coming out of the pubs. As they strode past The Crown four unruly lads wolf whistled July and made some chauvinistic comments. The four were used to this having worked in the hospital A&E, so they just ignored it and walked past. Three very young teenage lads were now stuttering across the road in front of them, they too shouted unpleasant comments. They were followed by a couple of older lads who couldn't walk straight. The four nurses were walking near them by the cinema now, where one of the lads fell into the gutter while the other lad laughed. Sharon saw him fall and was concerned so she went over to him, followed by Sue, Hilary and Judy. Two older, sober members of the public came to help. One was a blond lad who took a look at the lad who fell into the gutter and then said to the others who now came to help that he deserved all he gets if he can't take his drink.

Sharon was concerned though, she didn't think this was an alcohol related incident. The blond lad then noticed something under the young lad's body that had fallen out of his pocket, so rolled him slightly to reveal a needled syringe. The blond lad then shouted to everyone gathered to be careful as this guy was a druggie. Two members of the public took a few steps back with caution. However, Sharon being a nurse took a look at the type of needle on view and realised this wasn't a druggie but a diabetic who had had a 'hypo' due to low blood sugar. Sharon went into nurse mode and with the help of Hilary propped the lad up and gave the lad one of her sugary fruit pastilles to combat the hypo."

"Soon the lad became conscious and the few members of the public who had come over to see the incident were shocked to see him get up, seemingly back to normal, and they realised that he was not drunk. In fact, he hadn't drunk a drop of alcohol but simply came out of the cinema, not realising that he was about to have a 'hypo' and collapsed in the gutter. The blond lad apologised to him for assuming he was a druggie. Then everyone went their way. Hilary laughed. Nurses never get a break."

Uncle Chris continued with a smile on his face. The grandchildren knew the twist was coming but couldn't work out what it would be.

"They all continued their way to Costa. As they walked down Oxford Street Sue wanted to stop off for some cigarettes and Hilary mentioned a need to stop at Boots the chemist for some essentials. The other two went straight into Costa and got the cappuccino's in for them all. After getting her cigarettes, Sue joined Judy and Sharon in Costa. "

"Hilary finished at Boots and then walked towards Costa to join the others. On the way, there was an old lady sitting outside the Women's Institute Late Night Respite Centre. Hilary smiled to the old lady and said "Hi".

The old lady asked if Hilary was coming into the Institute, but Hilary just smiled.

He then said

"I can't. Only ladies can go in there I'm afraid, and I'm a bloke".

The old lady smiled and said "We need nice men like you in our world. I like your flashy white trousers by the way".

Uncle Chris leant back in his chair by the fireside and gulped some more whisky.

Ash and Sandy looked at each other.

Ash said "I didn't realise that Hilary was male, I thought he was female"

Sandy agreed. "Yes, I thought he was female too, which is a bit bad really as both you and I are female as well." as Ash and Sandy stared at each other.

Uncle Chris smiled. The two girls had been fooled again.

The End

Dedication

My thanks go to Chris for his wonderful help, Jade for being Ellie's bestie and the lovely Watsons for their thoughts.

If you enjoyed these short stories please let the publisher know, as a second volume of Uncle Chris's Collection of Crafty Short Stories is on its way.......

Money raised will contribute to worldvision.org.uk/support who support vulnerable children worldwide, especially in Ukraine.